Note to Readers

The American Adventure continues in *Danger in the Harbor*. While the Smith family is fictional, the events that surround this story are not. Queen Anne's War and the Great Fire left Boston with major problems. Many people went hungry, and some grain merchants sold their goods to other colonies, creating bread shortages. The riots that are featured in this story actually happened.

Just as we must do today, the people who lived in Boston in 1713 had to discover ways to solve their differences peacefully.

DANGER *in the* HARBOR

JoAnn A. Grote

BARBOUR
PUBLISHING, INC.
Uhrichsville, Ohio

ISBN 1-57748-147-X

Published by Barbour Publishing, Inc., P.O. Box 719, Uhrichsville, Ohio 44683
http://www.barbourbooks.com

Member of the
Evangelical Christian
Publishers Association

Printed in the United States of America.

Cover illustration by Peter Pagano.
Inside illustrations by Adam Wallenta.

CHAPTER ONE
Fire!
Boston 1713

Beth Smith raced down Union Street toward the waving wall of orange and yellow flames. They lit the night with their awful color. The roar and crackle was louder than anything she'd heard in her ten years of life.

Her heart thudded so loud it sounded like the hoofs of a horse racing down a street. For as far as she could see, the ground, sky, and everything in between was nothing but flames. Houses, shops, and churches she'd passed cheerfully only a few hours ago were framed against the eerie, burning light.

Cornhill, Queen Street, and King Street were all ablaze, and the fire was coming closer, where Dock Square met Union Street. She could feel the heat through her cotton nightgown. How could such a huge fire exist so close to the harbor, where there was so much water that hundreds of ships couldn't hide its surface?

Terror surged through her veins. Were the flames going to engulf all of Boston? She should turn around and flee to her home. There were still blocks of buildings between Dock Square and her house which weren't burning yet. She might be safe at home.

But the flames were as fascinating as they were frightening. She couldn't tear her gaze from the scene, and she kept moving toward the horrible sight. Besides, she had to find Martha.

A man with a wooden bucket bumped into her, knocking her to the ground. Water sloshed over her, cooling her from the fire's heat. She struggled to her feet and hurried on.

The street around her was filled with people rushing about madly. Some were carrying wooden and black leather buckets of water toward the flames. Some were throwing water on their homes and shops, hoping to keep them from burning if the flames came any closer. Other people were pulling pieces of furniture from their homes, piling them in carts or carrying them on their backs in hopes of saving some of their possessions. Dogs, cats, pigs, chickens, geese, and horses were as frightened as people, running in the direction from which Beth had come.

Everyone seemed to be shouting, but Beth couldn't hear the words. The fire's terrible roar drowned out the voices.

The flames were moving closer. If she was going to turn around, she should do it now. But the fire was sure to claim her father's cabinetmaker's shop. The flames had probably already destroyed it. She'd know as soon as turned the next corner. She had to see. Martha, her best friend, lived in the rooms above the shop. She had to be sure Martha had escaped.

Her eyes were stinging now from the heat and smoke. Burning bits of ash filled the air. Some landed on her nightgown, and she brushed them away with her hands, barely noticing their heat against her fingers. She was surprised to find her gown, which had been drenched clear through only minutes earlier, was now as dry as when she'd put it on. The ash left small holes with black edges in the cloth, but she paid them no mind.

Beth turned the corner and felt as though her chest had been gripped in giant hands. Her father's shop and all the buildings around it were on fire. She struggled through the crowded street, dodging people and animals and piles of belongings and burning bits of the buildings which had fallen to the street.

Thunder sounded as a building crashed into the fire. The fall sent a fresh shower of huge, glowing embers through the air, and once again Beth had to knock them from her gown and blonde hair.

She searched the soot-covered faces about her, looking for Martha. And then she saw her, in the window above the shop, her mother and little brother Samuel beside her. Fear rooted Beth's feet to the ground. The hair on her head felt as if it stood straight up beneath her cotton nightcap as she stared at the window.

Someone had to save them! Beth started grabbing people in

the street, pulling on their arms, trying to get them to stop, yelling at them, even though she knew they couldn't hear her.

But they only pushed her away and raced on about their own business.

She turned back to look again. Martha had climbed out the window and was hanging there, her hands on the sill. And then she let go and started to fall.

Beth screamed and screamed and screamed. . .

"Beth, you're safe now." A soft voice broke through the awful screams, and someone shook her. A moment later Beth opened her eyes, and the terrible sights faded away. Her older sister, Mary, lay beside her. Concern filled the eyes which were as blue as her own. "You were having that dream again."

Beth sat up and pushed aside the quilt. "Yes." This time it was a dream. But a year-and-a-half ago it had been real. The 1711 fire had been the worst fire in the colonies since the first people came to America from Europe.

She brushed the hair back from her forehead. It was damp with sweat.

A rooster crowed in the yard below their window. Day was beginning to edge away the darkness in the room.

"First light." She pushed herself to the edge of the feather bed she and Mary shared. "I'd best get breakfast."

Mary rubbed a hand lightly over Beth's shoulder. "Are you all right?"

Beth nodded. "It was only a dream."

Only a dream, but it had changed her life and that of her family. Her gaze rested on the oval frame, which hung on the wall, with the pen-and-ink drawing of Mary's husband, Rob Allerton.

The Great Fire and the war together changed our lives, she thought, *and those of everyone in Boston.*

Rob had been killed a year before the fire, in the battle with the French for Port Royal in Nova Scotia. He never even saw his and Mary's first and only child, who was born three months later. Mary had named the child Robert after his father.

Reaching for her petticoat, she heard little Robert stir in his small bed. "Did I scream when I was dreaming and wake him?"

Mary pulled the quilt up around his chin. "You didn't frighten him. He's almost asleep again."

Beth heard stirring in the room beside them and quickly finished dressing. Her mother's soft footsteps passed in the hallway as Beth tucked her white neck scarf around the top of her blue calico gown. Had her screams or the roosters awakened the rest of the people in the house? The nightmares were embarrassing. No one else in the house had bad dreams about the fire.

She tied her long, brown, everyday apron over her dress as she hurried down the stairs to the first floor hallway, through the dining room, and into the kitchen. *At least the fire never reached our home,* she thought. It was a fine house, with a kitchen and two large rooms downstairs and four bedchambers on the second floor, but not so grand as the homes of wealthier merchants.

Normally Beth didn't like getting up before the men in the house to help her mother get breakfast. Today she was glad to have something to do to put the dream's awful pictures from her mind.

There was a chill in the April morning air when she slipped into the back yard, and she pulled her woolen scarf about her shoulders. In spite of the chill, she liked the smell of the soft sea air from the nearby harbor.

Her mother was already feeding the chickens and geese that roamed free about the town, returning always to their yard to roost in the evening. One old gander hurried over to Beth, pulling at her apron with his beak in the hope she'd have more food. She shooed him away and carried her empty wooden bucket over to the cow. She waved at the neighbors, who were busy feeding their own fowl.

"Are you having a fine morning, Millie?" She patted the brown cow and settled on the short, three-legged stool beside it. Leaning against the cow's warm side, she began milking.

The family's gray tabby cat came running across the yard, perched her front paws on the edge of the bucket, and lapped at the stream of warm milk with her pink tongue. Laughing, Beth pushed her away. "You'll have yours when I'm done."

Her mother was stirring up the coals in the dining room fireplace, and Beth had just finished setting the table with heavy pewter plates and mugs, when her father and the three boys entered the room. All of them wore the coarse, wide-sleeved shirts and leather knee breeches, covered by leather aprons they wore for work in her father's cabinetmaker's shop.

Her father settled himself in the tall-backed chair beside the fireplace with the Bible, as he did every day while waiting for the morning meal to be served, and read silently. She noticed his hands, as she always did. The skin was pink and white with scars from the fire she'd seen in her dream.

William stretched his long, thin frame, ran his fingers through his straight blond hair, and yawned. Beth grinned. Her fourteen-year-old brother never woke up quickly like she did.

She was heading back toward the kitchen to fetch bread when

Tim's grating voice stopped her. "Heard you screamin' like a banshee this mornin', Beth. Have another nightmare?"

Beth clenched her apron in her fists, took a deep breath, and turned to face him. "You don't even know what a banshee is, Timothy Cutter. But if one saw that strange looking, curly brown hair of yours, it would scream for sure."

She didn't know what a banshee was either, but she wouldn't admit it to Tim for the world. Her father's youngest apprentice was two years older than William but acted younger, in Beth's opinion. He hardly ever spoke to her unless it was to tease, and his teasing always held a mean streak.

"Let's not begin the day with unkind words." Her father spoke in his usual quiet voice, but both she and Tim knew better than to continue. Her father expected to be obeyed without raising his voice.

"Tim, it would be a good thing if you went to North Square for fresh water before the day's work begins." Mr. Smith made it sound like a suggestion instead of the order they all knew it to be.

"Yes, sir."

"See you hurry. Breakfast will be on the table soon."

Tim headed for the kitchen to get the buckets and yoke. Beth stared after him. She much preferred it when the apprentice boys had lived in a room at the back of the shop before the Great Fire. It was bad enough to wait upon her brother and father, without being expected to wait on the apprentices, also.

She stopped beside Will, who was looking out the window. When Tim had entered the kitchen, she whispered, "I don't see how you can bear that Timothy Cutter!"

"He's not so bad. If you didn't show such a temper, he wouldn't tease you so much."

"Don't you even mind sharing your bedchamber with him and Charles?"

Will's narrow shoulders lifted his work shirt in a shrug. "I rather like it. It's like having brothers."

"Well, I liked it better when they slept in the room behind the old shop. And you wouldn't think they were so wonderful if you were the one who had to prepare their meals and wash and mend their clothes."

He didn't seem to mind anything about the way the Great Fire and Queen Anne's War had changed their lives, she thought, stalking into the kitchen. Will liked working in their father's shop, learning the cabinetmaker's skills. He would have been doing the same thing regardless of the things that had happened to them.

She slammed the round loaf of rye bread onto a pewter plate. It was her life that had changed most. She missed dame school. Not that she missed Goodwife Higgins, who tried so hard to teach her to sew a fine seam, but she did miss talking and laughing with the other girls. Now she spent her days helping about the house and watching little Robert while Mary worked with the dressmaker.

She almost ran right into Charles when he entered the kitchen. He caught the round of bread as it slipped from the plate she tipped to avoid hitting him.

At twenty, Charles was no taller than Will, but he was much broader. His long dark hair wasn't a mass of tight little curls like Tim's, and his tongue wasn't as sharp. A kind smile always twinkled in his dark brown eyes.

"Don't mind Tim," he said, setting the bread back on the plate in her hands. "Everyone has bad dreams sometimes. Even Tim."

12

Her anger began to melt. She didn't really mind Charles living with them, she admitted to herself. "Do you ever have bad dreams?"

"Of course."

"Do you dream about the fire? You would have been killed in it if you hadn't wakened in time to save yourself and Tim."

"No, I don't dream about the fire. I dream about London after my parents died when I was ten, and about the trip across the ocean on the ship. There were some bad storms. I didn't think I'd ever see Boston."

"Do you wake up screaming?"

"No, but the dreams are bad, just the same."

Mrs. Smith bustled into the room. "What is the matter with you this morning, child? The day will be half gone before we've eaten."

Beth hurried to bring the simple meal of bread and milk to the table, giving Charles a thank-you smile for his kind words.

Tim returned from the well just in time for the meal. Everyone stood respectfully behind their chairs while Father led them in grace. He made special mention of the bread in his prayer, and Beth remembered that grain and bread were scarce in Boston now.

When everyone had eaten, Beth passed the voider, a large wooden bowl, around the table. Each person put their used wooden or pewter bowls and wooden noggins from which they'd drunk their milk, into the voider, and Beth carried it to the kitchen where she would wash them later.

Her father was handing the Bible to Will when she returned to the table. Each morning one of the children in the household read a bit of Scripture. Mr. Smith reminded them often that the law required adults to see that the children in their homes learned to read, so they could know what the Bible said. He'd seen to it that all the children had gone to school to learn to read. Though none of them were in school any longer, he was determined they should practice their skills and not hear the Bible read only on Sundays.

"Read Matthew 22:34-39, William," he instructed.

Beth was glad he selected Will to read. Will had more schooling than the rest of them, since her father expected Will to take over his cabinetmaker's shop one day. She liked to listen to Will read. He never stumbled over the words like she and the others did.

Will stood up and began reading. She enjoyed listening to the sound of his voice and didn't pay attention to the words until he read, " 'Thou shalt love the Lord thy God with all thy heart, and with all thy soul, and with all thy mind. This is the first and great commandment. And the second is like unto it, Thou shalt love thy neighbor as thyself.' "

Could anyone love other people as much as they loved themselves? Beth wondered. She squirmed uneasily in her seat. The verses made her uncomfortable. Maybe she loved her family as much as herself, but not other people, not even her best friend, Martha. Sometimes she even wished she had enough money to think of no one but herself.

"The verses Will read will be your memory verses this week, children." Mr. Smith stood up.

Chairs scraped against the wooden floor as everyone rose to start their workday.

Her father and the boys went across the hall to the other side

14

of the building. Mr. Smith hadn't had the money to rebuild the shop that burned, so the family had had to give up the use of the large sitting room. It was now Mr. Smith's shop. He said if they watched their spending very carefully, maybe he could rebuild the shop in a few years. Beth hoped so.

Mary kissed little Robert, told him to be a good boy for Beth, and left for her day's work at the dressmaker's.

Mrs. Smith hooked a large basket covered with a linen cloth over her arm and slipped a small leather bag into the pocket beneath her apron. "I'm going to take the cow to the common to graze and then go to the market to purchase fresh meat for dinner. Don't forget, you need to work in the garden this morning. See that you watch Robert carefully."

The door closed behind her, and the room was suddenly very quiet. The emptiness made Beth feel lonely and depressed.

She wished her mother weren't taking Millie, the cow, to the common. Normally that was Beth's chore, and one of her favorites. It gave her a chance to get away from the house and feel like she had some freedom.

Beth sighed and smoothed her apron. Another day of work. When she was grown, she wasn't going to live like this. She'd marry a wealthy young merchant, live in a fine house with servants, wear beautiful clothes, and travel—maybe to England.

Her daydream ended when Robert yanked on her apron. "Beth, let's play."

There would be no play for her today. The thought made her tired. She took Robert's small hand in her own and went out to the garden.

15

CHAPTER TWO
The Accident

Beth patted the black earth into a small hill, burying the seeds that would bring the family's food for the coming year. Corn, pumpkin, and beans were all planted in the same hill. This summer, the pumpkin's green vines with yellow trumpet-shaped blossoms and golden-orange pumpkins would wind pleasantly between corn stalks. The beans would climb the corn stalks as they would a pole.

But right now, there was only the black earth. Beth stared at her hands in disgust. The nails were cracked from pushing at the dirt that was caked beneath them. Would she ever have nice soft hands with shiny buffed nails like the wealthy ladies in town?

A barrel of dead fish stood at one side. She kept the wooden cover on the barrel when she wasn't reaching inside it, but even that couldn't hide the awful smell. Large black flies buzzed constantly about the barrel. She had to place one fish in each hill of dirt to fertilize the seeds. It was the part of the chore she hated most.

She had to admit, in spite of disliking the work, that it would be nice to have fresh vegetables again soon. She was tired of eating only dried vegetables and fruit.

At a furious cackling and flutter of wings, she turned her head sharply. "Robert, stop chasing the chickens!"

The two-year-old stopped in his tracks, looked at her with wide, innocent brown eyes beneath his long brown hair, and stuffed a dirty thumb in his mouth. The chickens scurried away gratefully, gathering beneath the apple and cherry trees near the fence.

Beth got up from her knees and hurried over to Robert. "Take your thumb out of your mouth. Every day I have to tell you not to put dirty things in your mouth."

He gave her a wide, angelic grin. "Rob love Beth."

Her impatience whooshed out of her in a sigh. She knelt in front of him and gave him a big hug. "Beth loves Robert, too." She never could stay angry with him when he turned that smile on her.

"Come, Robert. You can help me plant the garden." Taking his

17

hand, she led him back to the hoed dirt. "See this basket with the dried up yellow kernels? That's corn. And these big flat seeds are pumpkins. The small ones in this small basket are beans. When I ask you for a seed, you hand me the kind I ask you for. Do you understand?"

Robert nodded his fat little face until his straight brown hair bounced.

"Good." About three feet from the last hill, she hoed the dirt into another hill. Holding her breath, she reached into the barrel for another fish and dropped it into the small hole she'd made in the top of the hill. "Hand me three corn kernels, Robert." She held out her hand.

Nothing landed in it.

She looked up at Robert. His face was screwed into a painful looking scowl. He was trying for all he was worth to break one of the hard kernels between his tiny baby teeth.

Beth grabbed his arm. "No, Robert! Those aren't for eating. They're to be put in the ground."

Robert dutifully handed her the wet kernel. "Why?"

"Because that way it can grow into a large corn stalk, taller than you, taller than your grandfather, even. Lots of corn kernels will grow on it. Then we can cook them, and they'll be soft and taste much better than these hard old things."

"Why?"

She bit her lips hard together to keep from making a smart reply and dropped the kernels into the ground. "Because that's the way God makes corn grow."

"Oh." Robert carefully chose another kernel and held it out to her. "Why?"

"So you would have something to ask questions about."

He smiled broadly. "God loves Rob?"

"Yes. Now give me a pumpkin seed."

He looked at the three baskets and frowned.

"This one, Robert. The pumpkin seeds are large and flat. See?"

He nodded and handed her another one.

"Thank you. Next we'll need the beans, from the smallest basket."

He giggled while she buried the pumpkin seeds. *Now what had she said that he found so funny,* she wondered. She turned about.

"Oh, no!" Two large geese had their long black beaks in the flat basket of dried corn. "Shoo!" The birds ignored her.

Beth jumped to her feet and waved her brown apron at them. "Shoo! You've already been fed!"

One goose waddled away, protesting loudly. The larger one let out a long "ho-o-onk," wound his skinny neck around, nipped at the edge of her apron, and caught it fast. "Oh, you! Let go, you pesky old thing!"

Robert was no help to her. He just stuck another dirty finger in his mouth and giggled until he was rocking back and forth.

Beth tugged at her apron. The goose tugged back.

Beth took firmer hold with both hands, pressed her lips together, and tugged as hard as she could. The goose let go. "Oof!" Beth landed smack in the middle of the hill she'd just been planting.

Robert's laughter pealed out. "Beth sat down!"

"Stupid goose," she muttered, pushing herself to her feet. She brushed vigorously at the back of her skirt to remove the dirt, then tried to repair the hill of seeds.

"Goosey is back," Robert announced cheerfully.

She shooed the bird away from the basket with the hoe this

time, careful to keep her apron out of his reach. "Just wait until its time to pluck your feathers. I'll get you then," she warned the honking creature.

She removed her apron and laid it over the basket of corn. "There. Now Goosey won't be able to eat any, will he, Robert?"

Robert dutifully shook his head.

But when she asked him for more seeds two more hills down the row, Robert didn't hand her any. "What now?" she muttered, turning around.

Robert was running along the fence, carrying her apron high in one arm. It fluttered out behind him, where Goosey chased it for all he was worth.

"Robert!"

He ignored her and kept running. Beth ran after him. It was her oldest, most ragged apron, but she didn't care to spend her evening mending it.

She finally retrieved it, scolding Robert smartly, and examined her apron. There were no new rips, though she couldn't see how it had escaped.

Retrieving from the kitchen a broom Will had made from a birch sapling, she handed it to Robert. "Why don't you sweep the back stoop while I finish planting?"

He went at it enthusiastically, his fat little arms pumping. Watching him, Beth grinned. The broom was so much taller than he was that it was difficult for him to sweep without falling over.

Beth put on her apron and went back to work. This time she kept the baskets on the other side of the hill, where she could see them.

She'd planted three more hills before she heard, "Yoo-hoo, Beth!"

Her friend Martha was hanging over the wooden gate at the back of the long yard. A thick braid of red-gold hair hung over her shoulder, and the front of her dress and tucker framed a face filled with freckles. Her green eyes were filled with friendliness as Beth hurried over to talk with her.

Martha's three-year-old brother, Samuel, with his mist of reddish-gold curls, was with her. Beth opened the gate for him. "Why don't you come in and say hello to Robert? He's sweeping the stoop, see?"

Sam nodded and ran to join him.

Beth rested her arms along the top of the gate. "I dreamed of you last night." A shudder ran through her. "I dreamed about the fire. But I woke up before Father and Will saved you. I'm so glad you didn't die in that fire, Martha."

"Me, too. Let's not think about it."

But Beth couldn't help but think about it for a minute or two longer. During the fire Beth had stared so hard at Martha hanging from the window that she hadn't seen Charles stumble out of the first floor of the shop pulling an unconscious Tim. She hadn't known her father and Will were only a few feet behind her in the street until they rushed forward to catch Martha. In only a couple minutes they had Martha, her little brother, Samuel, and her mother all safe.

"I delivered some bread to Judge Sewall's home and stopped to say hello to you on the way back to the bakery." Martha swung the empty basket for Beth to see.

"I guess rich people can always afford bread," Beth said.

Martha nodded. "At least with Mother working at the bakery, we never go hungry. But with grain and flour scarce, Baker Ames doesn't let us have as much bread as when it's plentiful."

"We haven't been eating much bread lately, either. But Mother tries to see that we have it at least once every other day. We have a lot of things made from ground corn and use lots of milk to make the grain and corn go further."

Beth followed Martha's gaze to where Robert and Samuel were giggling while Goosey nipped at a button on Robert's breeches. She knew she should chase Goosey away. If he tore Robert's breeches, she'd spend time that evening mending them.

Beth sighed and rested her chin on her arms. "I miss school days, don't you? Then we could giggle and play and not have to work all day."

"Except at learning to read, sew, and do fancy needlework."

Beth wrinkled her nose. "You're right. I'm glad we don't have sewing lessons every day."

"I rather miss school. I liked sewing and reading. Now I never have time to read, and the only sewing I do is to mend worn out, torn clothes."

"I have to mend my clothes and the boys' things, too. It's the worst of all the chores." Beth frowned down at her dirt-filled, torn nails. "Even worse than planting."

Martha smiled. "It could be worse. If we lived on the frontier, we'd have to plant our gardens while our fathers and brothers guarded us with their muskets from attacks by the French and unfriendly Indians."

"You're right." Beth felt a little ashamed for complaining so much. Martha's life was much more difficult than her own, yet it was Martha who always cheered her up. She never complained.

"I must hurry back." Martha called over the fence, "Come, Samuel! We must leave." She turned back to Beth. "Mother isn't well, so she hasn't been able to do all her work at the bakery. Mr.

Ames, the baker, said I must do some of her work, in addition to my own chores and watching Samuel."

Beth waved at the two as they walked off down the narrow alley between the tall, closely built houses. Robert stood in the open gate and called "goo'bye" to Samuel.

Martha and her mother had had to work so hard at Mr. Ames's bakery since her father died. At least they hadn't had to go to the almshouse, which Boston had built for its poor people near the common and burying ground. She knew the town fathers had good intentions with the almshouse, but with Queen Anne's War and the Great Fire, it was overflowing with widows and children. Due to the money the town and colony had to spend on the war, the town couldn't afford a jail, so prisoners were also kept at the almshouse. A shudder ran through Beth at the thought. She wouldn't like to think of Martha and Samuel in that place.

Since Mrs. Lankford worked for Mr. Ames, he let her and the children live in the room at the back of the bakery. The room was small and dark, and Beth hated to visit Martha there. Not that she stopped often. Mr. Ames didn't like Martha's friends stopping to see her.

A strange sound broke in on Beth's thoughts. Robert pulled on her apron. She looked down at him impatiently. Her blood froze.

Robert's round face was purple, his brown eyes wide as plates. One pudgy little hand circled his neck. His mouth was open wide, but only strange tiny sounds came out.

He was choking!

CHAPTER THREE
Will Father Sell?

Beth pounded her flat hand against Robert's back. Nothing happened. She pounded it again, over and over until she lost count of how many times. Nothing changed.

She thought her chest would burst from fear. What should she do? "Help us, Lord!" she cried.

Grabbing Robert about the waist, she turned him upside down and hit his back again right between his shoulder blades, hard, with her fist. Nothing happened.

She hit his back again. Something popped out of his mouth.

Beth stood him on his feet. He was taking large gasps of air, his dark wool jacket heaving over his chest. The awful purple color was leaving his face. He was so weak that he swayed and grabbed at her apron to keep his balance, but he was breathing.

"Thank You, Lord," Beth whispered, hugging Robert fiercely.

"Rob, whatever did you swallow?" She reached into the sparse early spring weeds and picked up the item she'd seen fly out of his mouth. "A stone! How many times have I told you not to eat stones? You mustn't put everything in your mouth. Shame on you, Robert!"

Robert's eyes filled with tears, and his bottom lip jutted out. "It hurt, Beth."

"That's why you're not supposed to eat stones."

A tear rolled down his cheek. "Don't you love Rob any more?"

She wiped his tear away, the dirt from her thumb leaving a muddy smudge across his cheek. "Of course I do." She hugged him close. "I only got mad because I don't want you to be hurt."

He put a grubby little hand against her own cheek. She always liked the feel of his baby hands on her face. They made her feel special. "Beth hurt, too?"

Puzzled, she frowned at him. "No."

"Why Beth crying?"

She put both hands to her face. It was wet with tears. She hadn't even realized she was crying. "I guess I'm crying because I love you so much."

His grin warmed her heart. *Thank You for not letting him die, Father God,* she thought.

It wasn't long before her mother came through the back gate

with fresh meat she'd purchased from a farmer who had come to town to sell meat to the townspeople. Robert dashed over to her and started telling the story of the stone he'd eaten.

Mother couldn't understand his story, so Beth had to explain it to her. Mother caught Robert up in her arms in spite of the heavy basket with the linen towel which hung at one elbow. She beamed at Beth over his shoulder. "You did very well, Beth."

Beth's stomach felt funny, but she felt proud at the same time. It was nice to hear her mother compliment her.

"You've done enough planting for the day, Beth. Come inside and help me prepare stew."

Beth was only too glad to do so. After washing her hands in the wooden trough in the yard, she hurried down the cellar to find the dried vegetables necessary for the dish.

The cellar with its earthen walls and floor was damp and cool and smelled musty. She noted that many of the baskets and barrels were almost empty after the long winter. The vegetables she was planting would fill the containers in the fall.

She dug into the sand in one huge barrel to remove a yellow squash and some carrots, grabbed a large onion from a nearby basket, then hurried up the shaky, narrow wooden stairs.

"Do you want me to get some beans, too?" she asked her mother, setting the colorful vegetables on the wooden work table in the kitchen.

"That's a good idea."

Beth hurried through the downstairs rooms and up the steps. The beans were funny, dried up green forms strung on linen thread hanging from the attic rafters where they wouldn't grow moldy as they would in the damp cellar. She remembered spinning the thread last summer and all the family stringing the beans on warm summer evenings. Beth had to climb around the dried corn piled on the floor to reach the area where the beans hung.

Her mother was chopping the meat into bite-size chunks when Beth entered the kitchen with a string of beans. She pushed the beans off the string and into the cast iron pot that would be used to cook the stew over the fire in the large kitchen fireplace.

Mrs. Smith had already stirred up the fire and put on logs which would have to burn down before the kettle could be hung on the large crane that held it over the flames. The stew would simmer all day long before it was ready.

"Now that spring is here, it won't be long until it's uncomfortable to cook in here again," Beth said. The room was beginning to get warm from the fireplace heat, but she knew she would be glad for the warmth after the sun went down and she had to clean up from the evening meal.

She found a strong knife and began to chop the carrots she'd brought from the cellar. The constant pounding from her father's shop on the other side of the house kept up a continual beat while she chopped. She'd leave the onion until last. It wouldn't need to cook as long as the hard carrots and squash. *Besides,* she thought, *onions always make my eyes burn and run with tears.*

She stepped on a low, three-legged stool. Even so, she had to stretch to reach the dried sage hanging upside down from the kitchen rafter. The herb with its long, narrow leaves added a nice flavor to stews. Her mother used herbs so often in her cooking that she chose to hang them in the kitchen instead of the shed or attic. Beth was glad. She liked the fragrances the dried herbs added to the kitchen.

"Where's Robert?" her mother asked, taking the sage leaves from Beth and crumbling them into the black pot.

Beth glanced quickly around the kitchen. He wasn't there. "I haven't seen him since you came home from market."

Mrs. Smith shook her head, a smile on her face. "That boy is always running off for new adventures. You'd best find him."

"Yes, Mother." Beth knew her impatience showed in her voice. It seemed she always had to interrupt what she was doing to look for Robert or look after him.

At least she knew he hadn't followed her to the attic or cellar. She tried the backyard first. He wasn't there or in the shed where her father stored wood for his business and her mother stored the dried herbs she hadn't space for on the kitchen and attic rafters.

Next she tried the second floor bedrooms. He wasn't there either. She hurried down the steep stairs, her slippers slapping softly against the wood. *I hope the rascal hasn't gone down the street,* she thought, her impatience growing. *Who would think such a little boy could be such trouble?*

She tripped over her skirt and threw herself against the wall to keep from falling. Lifting the skirts of her work dress and apron, she walked the rest of the way down the steps more slowly. She was always throwing her thoughts ahead of her feet and tripping! Why couldn't she learn to walk daintily like a lady, like her older sister Mary? People always commented on Mary's grace. They laughed over Beth's clumsy ways.

When she reached the bottom of the steps, she turned into her father's shop on the other side of the house from the kitchen and dining room. As soon as she opened the door, the pounding she heard all day long grew louder. The sweet smell of trimmed woods and sawdust greeted her.

"A visit from the lady of the house!" Curly-haired Tim grinned across the room at her. He was holding a large door to a cabinet

28

while Charles hammered nails into the beautifully designed brass hinge that would hold the door securely.

Beth wrinkled her nose at him and looked around the room. Her father was carefully measuring a piece of wood.

A soft "whir" caught her attention. The large wheel—taller than her father and about four feet in diameter—attached to the lathe turned slowly. Will was standing behind the wheel, but no one was working the lathe. She frowned at him. What could he be doing?

The wheel slowed, then gained a little speed once more, the "whir" growing stronger. Someone giggled.

Beth walked through the thin layer of sawdust, remembering to lift her skirts, and peered over a wide work table. There, standing with both feet on the paddle that ran the huge wheel, was Robert, giggling for all he was worth.

He jumped off the wooden paddle, which the boys and men in the shop ran with only one foot. The "whir" slowed as the wheel slowed.

"Watch me, Beth!" He jumped back on with both feet. Will stood behind him, his arms out to catch him if he tripped. But Robert didn't trip. He just giggled as the paddle slowly lowered under his weight and the wheel gained a bit of speed again. When the paddle reached the floor, he jumped off, and the paddle slowly raised.

"See, Beth? I made the wheel go!" He pointed a pudgy finger at it.

"I see." She couldn't help but smile at him. He was having so much fun. "Are you teaching Will how to do it?"

"No. Will teaching me," Robert answered seriously.

Will brushed his straight hair off his forehead and gave Beth a lazy grin. "I have to admit, I've never tried his method. I only use one foot on the paddle."

"You can do it, Uncle Will," Robert assured him. "Like this." He jumped back on the paddle. "See?"

"I see. But I think my feet are too big to do it your way."

Robert jumped off the paddle and placed one of his little feet beside Will's. "Oh. You has big feet, Uncle Will."

"You shouldn't be in here bothering the men and keeping them from their work, Robert," Beth scolded.

Her father looked over at the boy and smiled. "We don't mind him stopping in for a few minutes."

"Only natural a boy wants to spend time with men instead of girls," Tim called across the room.

Beth gave him what she hoped was a withering look. Men, indeed! As if anyone would prefer his mean company to any girl's.

"Besides," Will was saying, "Robert might want to be a cabinetmaker one day, like his grandfather and uncle, and like his father used to be. Isn't that right?"

Robert nodded his head until his hair bounced.

"When we visit the wharf, he wants to be a sailor," Beth reminded him. "When we visit Mr. Franklin at the candleshop, he wants to be a candle maker. And when we go to church, he wants to be a preacher. Who knows what he'll be when he grows up?"

Her father's rich laugh boomed out. "She has you there, William."

She gave Will a superior smile and held out her hand to Robert. "Let's go."

"Have you spent any time with him on his lessons, Beth?" her father asked.

"No, I've been too busy with chores."

"Try to find a little time this afternoon. It's important he learn to read so he will be allowed into school when he's older."

"Yes, Father." *Robert wouldn't be entering school for three-and-a-half years,* she thought. The stew had to be ready to eat this evening, and the seeds had to be planted soon if they wanted any vegetables the rest of the year. Ever since she had to quit dame school herself, it seemed there was never enough time in the day for all the work that needed to be done.

"Can I have a apron like Uncle Will's?" Robert asked.

Beth bit back a groan. That's all she needed! Something else to sew, a leather work apron like the men wore in the shop. "Maybe when you're older."

"But, I want—"

The tinkle of a bell interrupted him. The sound meant some-one had entered the front door. Beth opened the shop door into the entryway to greet the customer.

A gentleman in a bright green knee-length coat trimmed with gold braid smiled down at her. Beth recognized him at once. Mr. Foy was a well-known merchant and ship owner in Boston.

Beside him stood his daughter, a girl only a couple years older than herself. Beth knew who she was, though they'd never met. Miss Alice Foy's fine dress made Beth feel shabby. She resisted the desire to pull off her own dirty work apron.

She drew herself up as straight and tall as possible. "May I help you, sir?"

But her father had come from the shop to see the visitor him-self. His voice came from behind her. "What can I do for you, Mr. Foy?"

Beth paid no attention to the talk between her father and

Gentleman Foy, but she stayed where she was in the entryway. She wanted a chance to study Miss Foy's gown. Mary had sewn some gowns for Mrs. Foy and Alice. Had this been one of them?

It was beautiful. Wide, delicate lace trimmed the edges of the elbow length sleeves and the square neckline. The material was the most beautiful blue Beth had ever seen. *The color of the periwinkle flowers along the back fence,* she thought. Sprigs of yellow and white flowers decorated the inner skirt, which showed like an upside down "V" from the waist to the hem in the front of the dress. The blue outerskirt stood out wide at Miss Foy's hips. Beth knew a wire hoop beneath the dress made it stand out in such a fashionable manner.

She wore a hoop beneath her own skirt, but it was much smaller. She would never be able to garden in a skirt as wide as Miss Foy's.

She smiled shyly at Alice. The girl smiled back brightly. Beth thought with a tinge of envy that Miss Foy had a calm air of self-confidence about her. She supposed that was natural, when she wore such a lovely gown and knew she looked beautiful.

She'd have to remember to make a drawing of the dress as soon as possible, so she could remember what it looked like. If she ever had another new dress, Beth wanted it to be like Miss Foy's.

"What an exceptionally fine table!"

At Gentleman Foy's exclamation, Beth's glance darted to the dining room table. She realized she must have left the door to the room open when she was looking for Robert.

"Thank you, Mr. Foy," her father was saying. She could hear the touch of pride in her usually modest father's voice. "My father made that. He was a fine cabinetmaker."

"Indeed he must have been. I don't know that I've seen such

32

a fine piece, even in the best homes in Boston."

Beth smiled, and a warmth spread through her chest. They did have some very nice pieces of furniture in their home, which was only natural since her father and grandfather had both been among Boston's best cabinetmakers.

With the financial struggles her father had faced because of the war and fire, much of their best furniture had been sold to raise funds. Beth had hated to see it sold. It hurt to know their family pieces were in other people's homes, while their parlor had been turned into her father's shop.

The man rocked back and forth on his shoes, arched his gray eyebrows, and looked at her father. "Is there any chance you'd sell that table, Mr. Smith? I'd pay you a fine price for it."

Beth caught her breath and looked at her father. He was staring at the dining room table, his bottom lip caught between his teeth. He crossed his arms over his chest and rubbed his chin.

She loved that table so much! Would he sell it?

CHAPTER FOUR
Midnight Mystery

Beth's mother appeared suddenly, her rounded figure filling the doorway between the dining room and entryway.

"Mr. Foy, how nice to see you," Mrs. Smith greeted him with a broad smile. She glanced at Alice. "Your daughter has grown into a lovely young woman."

She must not have heard Mr. Foy's offer to purchase the table, Beth thought, *or she wouldn't be so cheerful.*

"I was just telling your husband how much I admire your table, Mrs. Foy."

Mrs. Smith turned and beamed at the table. "Thank you. I

admit it means more to me than it probably should." She turned about again before he could continue.

It was like her mother to hurry about, Beth thought. She was never rude, but she thought time was a gift and that it was wrong to waste even a minute.

"I see you found Robert, Beth." She held out a hand. "Why don't you come help me in the kitchen, young man?"

Robert went with her eagerly, always ready for something new.

Beth's throat grew tight when her mother ran the fingers of one hand lightly over the satin-smooth table top as she and Robert passed through the dining room. Would the table still belong to them by dinner hour?

Her father spread his hands and smiled at Mr. Foy. "You can see how it is. I cannot ask my wife to part with something so dear to her. However, I would be glad to make you a table just like this one."

Mr. Foy's small smile dented his fat face with dimples. "I guess I shall have to be content with that."

Beth felt suddenly light hearted, as though a smile had spread all through her. She knew it must not have been easy to say no to Mr. Foy. The family could certainly use the money the table would bring, and her father had no way of knowing when he said no whether Mr. Foy would agree to have another table made instead.

Her father called to Will to bring the account book. While the men discussed how much the table would cost, of what wood it would be made, and when it would be completed, Will wrote down their decisions in the book with his quill pen. Beth held the clay ink bottle for him.

When their father walked Mr. Foy and Miss Alice to Mr. Foy's carriage, Tim leaned against the shop door frame and stared moodily through the front doorway after the Foys. His usually teasing green eyes were black with anger. "Another of those rich gentlemen who doesn't care about the poorer people in town."

Will's eyebrows raised slightly. "Mr. Foy? He seems a nice enough man. As a merchant and ship owner, his business has been hurt by Queen Anne's War like everyone else's. A number of his ships were robbed by French pirates."

"Well-deserved loss, I say."

"You don't mean that, Tim," Will said. "Besides, Mr. Foy's furniture orders and those of the other wealthy people in town are what keep Father in business."

"Maybe. But do they give a fig for the poor people, while they eat wonderful meals off the beautiful tables your father makes? Gentleman Foy is a good friend of Mr. Belcher, and you know what kind of man Mr. Belcher is."

Will shrugged. Beth knew he hated arguments. He liked things pleasant and peaceful.

"What kind of man is Mr. Belcher, Tim?" Beth asked.

"A thief, that's what."

Will laughed. "He is not!"

"Is so." Tim's chin jutted out stubbornly. "What else do you call it when a man sends a shipload of grain to another colony when there are people in Boston starving?"

"It may not seem right to us," Will said quietly, "but Mr. Belcher owns the grain. He has a right to sell it to whomever he chooses. He can get a better price elsewhere. Getting the most he can for his grain doesn't make him a thief."

"He's as good as one." Tim wasn't about to give in. "One of his ships, loaded with wheat and bread, is set to leave port tomorrow.

Don't be surprised if it doesn't."

"What is that supposed to mean?"

"You'll see." Tim stalked back into the shop. A moment later Beth heard the rasp of a saw and knew he'd gone back to work and was taking his anger out on the wood.

"Are there really people starving in Boston?" Beth asked Will.

"I don't think anyone is actually starving, but a good number are going to bed hungry at night. With the grain shortage, some families haven't had bread for weeks, or so I've heard Father and some of his customers say to each other."

"Then why doesn't Mr. Belcher sell them some wheat?" Mr. Belcher was a wealthy man. His fine carriage outshone Mr. Foy's.

"Like I told Tim, he wants more money than he can make here."

Beth knew she and her family were tired of eating bread only once every other day, but she hadn't realized there were families in town that hadn't eaten any bread for weeks.

Her stomach tightened painfully at the thought of how hungry those people must be with only meat and dried fruits and vegetables to eat. Nothing was as filling as bread. What kind of man was Mr. Belcher, anyway, that he would let people go hungry? A shiver of distaste ran through her.

Later that night, Beth ducked behind a large barrel that reeked of tobacco. Water, smelly with dead fish and garbage, lapped against the pier. She peeked around the barrel at the shadows that were Will and Tim.

What were they doing out at this time of night? she wondered for the twentieth time. The moon was already out. It had to be late.

They were arguing now, a little farther along the wharf. But she couldn't hear what they were saying. All she could hear were the wind, the steady roll of waves, and a couple loud sailors emerging from a tavern facing the bay.

She sneaked out from behind the barrel and hurried a few feet closer to the boys. There was another barrel to hide behind there. She headed for it.

"Oof!" She landed flat on the pier's wide boards, her head over the edge. The white frill of the waves danced many feet below. Hurriedly she sat up and looked to see what had tripped her. "Stupid rope," she muttered, shoving at the thick wet cord which still had seaweed tangled with it.

Four shoes appeared beside the coil of rope. Without moving, Beth looked up through her lashes. It was only Will and Thomas. She sighed with relief, wiggled the fingers of one hand in greeting, and smiled feebly. "Hello."

Tim's grin flashed in the moonlight, as white as the top of the waves against the ocean. "If it isn't graceful Beth. Tripping over your own feet again, I see."

She scowled at him and started to tell him what she thought of him.

Will spoke first. "What are you doing here?"

"What am I doing here?" Beth scrambled to her feet, almost tripping again over the thick rope. "I'd say the question is 'What are you two doing here?' We'll all be in trouble if the constable sees us."

"They'd have to catch us first," Tim said.

"That shouldn't be hard to do on a pier," Beth replied hotly. "Where would we run to? Or maybe you think we could just jump into the harbor and swim away."

Will held out an arm toward each of them. "Stop arguing, you two. Beth, why are you here?"

"I saw you sneaking out the front door. So I followed. I wanted to see where you were going at this hour." She glanced down at her dress. "Robert woke up when Mary and I went up to get ready for bed. Mary has to be at the seamstress's early tomorrow, so I stayed up with Robert. He'd finally fallen asleep when I heard you two leaving."

If it hadn't been for Robert, she would have been sound asleep in her nightdress when they left, and she would have missed this adventure, she thought.

Tim was staring toward the next pier. She followed his gaze. The water was black in the dark. Ships and smaller sloops were outlined against the moonlit sky. Masts without their sails stood like proud trees in the night.

Suddenly a light flashed at the end of the next pier, as though someone had lit a lantern and immediately extinguished it. "Did you see that?" she asked, pointing.

Another light flashed.

"It's time!" Tim whirled around.

"Time for what?" Beth asked.

"Time for what?" Will echoed.

Tim ran across the wide pier and started to descend the wooden ladder at its side. "Get in the boat."

"What boat?" Beth ran after him.

"What's this all about?" Will demanded from beside her.

"Will you get in the boat?" Tim demanded in a loud whisper from the bottom of the ladder.

"We can't go out on the harbor at this time of night," Will argued.

"Haven't you any sense of adventure?" Tim teased. "Hurry, or it will be too late."

"Too late for what?" Will asked as Beth started to descend the ladder. "Beth, what are you doing?"

"I'm getting in the boat." She hoped her voice wasn't shaking as badly as her legs. It seemed a long way down to the boat now that she was on the ladder. She hadn't realized it would be so scary!

"You can't do that!"

"Watch me!" She felt slowly below her for the next rung. "Besides, we can't let Tim go out on the water at night alone."

"I wanted Will along, not you." Tim's hands closed about her waist and lifted her the last foot to the boat, standing her on one of the wooden seats. "What am I going to do with a girl aboard in the dark?"

The boat bobbed about. Beth grabbed both Tim's arms to keep her balance. "I can watch that you don't run into anything." She wasn't about to be left out of the nearest thing to an adventure she'd had a chance for in her life.

"You'll probably fall overboard. You're clumsy enough on land. You could be positively dangerous on a boat."

Her face grew hot from anger. "You'd best be careful, or I might knock you overboard—accidentally, of course."

A moment later Will stepped into the boat, setting it to bobbing harder. He immediately took a seat.

"I thought you weren't coming," she teased.

"I can't let you go out on the harbor with just Tim. Father would never forgive me if he found out."

The thought sobered her. Their father would be furious if he knew what they were doing. "We won't tell him."

"Sit down," Tim ordered her. "Untie us, Will. Then lend me a hand with the oars."

Beth carefully lowered herself to the hard, backless seat. "It's damp!"

Will grunted, tugging at the huge knot in the wide, wet rope holding the boat to the pier. "Of course it's damp. We're on water."

She pulled her feet from the bottom of the boat. "Yuck! What's all that?"

"Water," Tim said impatiently. She saw his grin flash. "You don't want to know what's in it."

"Stop teasing her." Will dropped down beside Tim and grabbed one of the oars Tim had set up. "There's always water in the bottom of the boats, Beth. Don't worry about it."

She frowned down at the black water sloshing about at her feet. Her shoes and the hems of her dress and petticoat were soaked already. She placed one foot on each side of the boat's curved bottom, just above the water sloshing in the bottom, and grabbed the edge of the seat to keep her balance.

"Where are we going?" Will asked.

"Just keep rowing," Tim answered.

"What did you mean when you said it was time?" Beth asked.

"I meant it was time to get into the boat, of course."

"But what else?" Certainly he didn't think she and Will silly enough to accept that answer!

"Just thought it was a nice night to go rowing in the moonlight."

"Timothy. . ."

"Shhh. Voices carry over the water, you know."

He was right. Whatever they were doing out here, they didn't want to be discovered. She might as well enjoy the ride.

She leaned against the side, hanging onto the wooden edge, and looked at the water beside her. It was still black. It lapped quietly against the boat's hull. The boys' grunts and the creak of the oars mingled with the soft splash of the oars dipping into the water.

Beth smiled. It was peaceful and nice. She liked the way they were moving quietly about the usually busy bay. Before long, they were passing ships moored past the low tide line. It gave her a funny feeling to see the dark, quiet ships towering above them while they bobbed slowly past. Long wooden rudders that guided the ships extended up the middle of the high sterns.

"We aren't the only ones out tonight. Look." She pointed at a small skiff about the size of their own that floated across the moonlit path on the water. It was quite a ways from them, but the silhouette could be clearly seen. There were four men in it.

"Probably just sailors returning to their ship." Tim leaned against his oar handle. "Let's rest a few minutes, Will, and then head back."

Will stopped rowing. "Wasn't there something special you wanted to see out here?"

"I just wanted to see if we could get away with it. Doesn't it feel nice out here?"

It did feel nice with the soft breeze off the water and the quiet all around. But Beth felt like Will. She was sure Tim had something planned when they'd started out.

Beth watched the other small boat. Suddenly a shadow slipped over the side and disappeared into the water. She gasped. "Someone in that boat jumped into the water!"

Will and Tim started, but Tim said firmly, "Just like a girl, imagining things."

"I'm not imagining anything. Someone got into the water. There goes another!"

"I saw him, too!" Will leaned forward, as though it would help him see better through the darkness.

"Maybe they need help." Beth's heart beat a frantic pace. "Maybe we should row over there."

"They don't need any help," Tim said. "They probably just wanted to take a swim."

"It's too cold to swim." She'd been wishing she'd thought to bring her shawl, and he thought men were swimming for fun!

"Maybe they like to swim when the water's cold. Besides, their friends wouldn't have let them go into the water if there was any danger."

That sounded reasonable.

"The men in the boat are rowing away."

"It's probably just drifting, like we are."

"No, they're rowing. Let's go see if they need help."

"Do you think men would want help from a couple of kids?"

"But—"

"Beth, you're being silly. If the men are rowing, they're probably just rowing alongside the swimming men."

"Well, now it's too late," she complained. "I can't see them anymore. The boat's moved behind the large ship anchored there."

"Probably the boat the sailors work on. Likely they had a late night at the local pub before sailing tomorrow."

Perhaps Tim was right, she thought. Still, she had an uneasy feeling about that boat.

"Let's get back." Will took up his oar again. "The longer we're gone, the more chance that Father will find we're not in our beds."

"No, let's wait awhile longer," Tim urged. "It's too nice out here to go back yet."

Beth was sure he had some reason for staying out on the bay. It was growing cooler, and she was anxious to get back. Her gaze skimmed the water, watching for the boat they'd seen earlier.

Her watch was rewarded. "They're back."

"Who is back?" Will asked.

"Those men. It looks like they're all in the boat again."

"I told you there was nothing to worry about." Tim grabbed his oar. "Let's start back."

"Maybe it's not the same boat." Will pulled on his oar.

Maybe it wasn't, but Beth felt sure it was. She gripped the edge of the seat as the boys' efforts shot the boat through the waters. Shivers inched up her spine, shivers that had nothing to do with the harbor breeze. There was something strange about the men in that boat.

CHAPTER FIVE
Tim Speaks Out

"Why must I mend Tim's silly old shirt?" Beth plopped down on a three-legged stool with the shirt in one hand and a threaded needle in the other. Remnants of logs smoldered in the fireplace beside her, delivering the occasional snap or pop that was such a common background in their home. "You and Mary are both better at stitching than I am, Mother."

Mrs. Smith smiled calmly at her daughter over her own mending. "Which is the very reason you need the practice. It's important for a girl to sew well. After all, one day you'll have to make and mend your own family's clothing."

Not me! Beth didn't dare say it out loud, but she had no intention of spending her life sewing other people's clothes. The only way she knew to avoid it was to marry someone wealthy. Someone who could afford to buy her beautiful gowns, like the one Miss Alice Foy was wearing the other day.

Someone like Mr. Josiah Foy?

The entire family had been shocked yesterday when their father told them Mr. Foy had asked permission for his son, Josiah, to court Mary. When the surprise had worn off, Mary agreed.

No one in the family had expected anyone as wealthy as Josiah to call on Mary! His father owned Foy Shipping Lines.

"Beth, quit daydreaming and get back to work," Mrs. Smith admonished gently as Will and Tim entered the room. "The evening will be over before you finish that job."

Beth pressed her lips together and jabbed the needle into the cloth. "Ouch!"

"Did you stick yourself again?" Tim stood beside her, grinning.

"Yes." She darted him an angry look. "I'll have to wait for a few minutes before sewing now, so I don't bleed on your stupid shirt."

"Aw, poor little girl."

Beth shot to her feet. "You can just mend your own shirt."

"Stop bickering, children."

Beth gritted her teeth and sat back down. She hated it when her mother called them children.

"Beth," she continued, "you know mending is your chore. Timothy has his own to mind. But I must say, Timothy, the shirt has quite a nasty tear. How did you manage it?"

Beth made a face at Tim. Let him answer that!

"Tore it on some wood."

Beth snorted. It wasn't exactly a lie. He'd torn it on the ladder when he'd climbed from the boat to the top of the pier last night.

"Try to be more careful in the shop, Timothy."

"Yes, Mrs. Smith." He turned his back to her and wrinkled his nose at Beth.

Tim was disgusting enough on an ordinary day, and today was far from ordinary. They hadn't been caught sneaking back into the house the night before, but it seemed to Beth that her head had just touched her pillow before it was time to get up and start the day's work. She was so tired that she'd been short-tempered all day long.

Mother rose and went into the kitchen, and Beth spoke while she had the chance.

"It's not fair that I have to work tonight because of our adventure last night. It was your plan, Tim, and your shirt, and I end up mending it."

Tim dropped into the chair Mrs. Smith had just left, leaned until the chair balanced on its back feet, and put his hands behind his head. "That's what girls are supposed to do. You might as well stop sputtering about it."

"You boys make me sick. You have all kinds of occupations to select from. If you're apprenticed to a trade you don't like, you can ask to be apprenticed to another trade instead."

"But you can't change trades without the master's approval," Will reminded her. "Why do you think so many apprentices run away?"

"Perhaps the master's daughters chase the apprentices away so they don't have to do so much sewing!"

The boys chuckled.

Beth shot to her feet, dropping the shirt to the floor. "You wouldn't think it so funny if you were a girl. Girls have nothing to say about their future. We're expected to learn how to stitch, do it well, and love it besides."

Will and Tim grinned at each other.

"Oh, stop it! I hate it when you look at me like that."

"Like what?" Will's face looked completely innocent.

"Like you think you're better than me only because you're boys and I'm a girl."

She ignored their laughter and went back to her work. She was so angry she could hardly see what she was doing. Sewing was so boring. You had to sit still and stare at nothing but your work. Her mind always wandered, and her needle wandered right along with it until her stitches were uneven, or she'd sewn right through the material onto her own apron, or something equally maddening.

Beth heard the front door open, and a minute later Martha Lankford walked into the room. Beth stared at her in surprise. It was unusual for any children their age to be visiting at this time of the evening.

Even more unusual for them to be out on the harbor after dark, she thought, remembering her adventure with Tim and Will the night before.

Voices in the entryway told Beth that Martha had not entered the house alone. "Hello, Martha. Who is with you?"

"I met Mary and Mr. Josiah Foy just down the street. Mary said they'd been for a walk by the common. Your father met them in the entry." Martha smiled shyly at the boys while crossing the room.

Martha's brown dress was dull from wear and many washings.

Two white lines circling the skirt showed the hem had been let down twice as she grew, and the dress was too short again now. There was a very neatly mended spot on one wrist, and another on the opposite elbow. Beth's dresses were old and worn, too, but she didn't think any of them looked as thin as Martha's.

Martha knelt on the floor beside Beth. "What are you working on?"

Beth darted a dirty look at Tim. "I'm just mending Tim's shirt."

Martha reached for the shirt and examined Beth's stitches. "The mend will be stronger and the shirt look better if you use smaller, more even stitches."

Beth jerked it back from her, resenting her friend's suggestion, even though it was kindly given. "I don't care how his shirt looks. I only know the mending will be done sooner if I use large stitches."

Martha shook her head, the waves of her pale red hair glinting in the firelight. "I doubt you shall ever become a seamstress."

"I should hope not!" Beth's mother, Mary, and Goodwife Higgins, her dame school instructor, had all tried to teach her to stitch properly. She simply hadn't the patience for it. Martha, on the other hand, loved to sew and did it well.

Mrs. Smith bustled into the room from the kitchen. "Why, Martha! What are you doing here so late?"

Martha rose to her feet respectfully. "Good evening, Mrs. Smith. My mother asked me to come. She isn't feeling well and must rest. Baker Ames says I must help all day in the bakery until she is better. Mother wondered whether Beth could watch Samuel while I work?"

"Of course she can. I hope your mother will feel better soon."

Beth bit back a groan. It was hard enough to complete her

chores every day while watching Robert. She wouldn't get anything done watching two boys!

"Is that Mary and Mr. Foy I hear in the entryway?" Mrs. Smith asked, removing her work apron hurriedly. "Will and Thomas, bring some apple cider and mugs. Don't dawdle now." She patted at her hair and frowned at the tallow candle and its flickering light on the small table beside Beth's chair. "I do wish we had some proper bayberry candles."

Was she embarrassed to have wealthy Josiah Foy in their home? Beth wondered.

Martha drew her thin brown shawl about her shoulders. "I'd best leave. Mother will be looking for me."

She slipped out as Mr. Smith, Charles, Mary, and Mr. Foy came into the room. A minute later the boys returned with a pitcher, and Mrs. Smith poured cider for everyone.

Mary laid a packet on the table. "Mr. Foy has brought a pound of sugared almonds. I'm sure he wouldn't object to my sharing his kind gift."

Mr. Foy clasped his hands behind his back. "The gift is yours to share in whatever manner gives you pleasure, Mrs. Allerton."

Beth noticed Mary's cheeks grow red at his words. Mary had told her it seemed strange to have another man call. She'd refused other suitors in the two years since her husband died.

Mary smiled across the room at her. "What are you working on, Beth?"

"Just mending."

Mary turned to Josiah. "Beth doesn't care for stitching, but she has a fine hand for drawing. When my husband died, she gave me a lovely drawing of him."

"May I see it?"

50

Mary must have been as surprised at his request as Beth was, for she stumbled a bit in agreeing before asking Beth to fetch it for her from their room.

Minutes later Beth handed the small framed pen-and-ink drawing to Josiah shyly.

"Your sister spoke truly. You have quite a talent, Miss Beth. My sister Alice paints scenes on glass, but she hasn't the eye of an artist as you have."

"Thank you, sir," she mumbled, feeling both proud and embarrassed.

"Has Robert been put to bed?" Mary asked.

"Yes. He could hardly keep his eyes open this evening," Beth said. "And no wonder, as he ran me ragged today trying to keep up with him."

"I have a son, too," Josiah said. "He's one-and-a-half. His name is Thomas."

So young Mr. Foy was a widower. *He and Mary seemed too young to have both lost their marriage partners,* Beth thought.

"Won't you sit with us for awhile, Mr. Foy?" Father asked. "I've a copy of the *Boston News Letter.* The children always read the articles aloud to us. I hate them to lose an opportunity to read."

Josiah inclined his head slightly. "I should like to join you, sir."

Father invited Josiah to be seated in the best chair in the house, the one Father usually used himself, with the high back and arms. It even had a leather seat cushion. The other chairs had no arms or cushions, and their seats were of wood or rush.

Bitterness stabbed at Beth's heart. They used to have more nice chairs, but their father had sold them. She bet the Foys were never so poor that they had to sell their family's furniture.

While Tim read in his usual jerky manner, Beth studied Josiah.

He was a tall man with a back as straight and firm as the back of the wooden chair in which he sat. He wore a white wig like those so popular among wealthy and powerful men. Parted in the middle, the wig waved from the top of his head to below his shoulders. His long red coat was trimmed with gold. Its deep white cuffs and collar were embroidered in gold. His breeches and silk shirt were white, and the knee-length white vest or waistcoat was finely embroidered with white thread. Even the white socks which came up over his knees were of silk.

Father and Will never dressed so elegantly. Neither had Mary's first husband, Robert Allerton. Rob had been an apprentice in her father's shop before they married and had been like an older brother to Beth and Will. He hadn't worn a wig but had had thick dark hair and big brown eyes like his son, little Robert. His eyes had usually been filled with friendly laughter.

Beth hadn't seen Josiah laugh or even smile once. Still, he seemed kind enough. He had brought Mary the sugared almonds, which were awfully good, and he had complimented her on her drawing. And when he looked at Mary, his rather stiff expression seemed to soften somewhat.

Beth glanced at Mary. What did she think of Josiah, this man who was so different from her first husband?

Tim handed the paper to Will. The first words Will read caught her attention. "Vandalism on Captain Belcher's ship."

Belcher! That was the man Tim had accused yesterday of being a thief for sending away grain and bread that townspeople needed. She forgot all about Josiah and Rob and listened to Will.

" 'Captain Belcher's ship was unable to leave Boston harbor this morning as planned. Last night, under cover of darkness, the ship's rudder was cut off. Captain Belcher ordered a new rudder made at a local shipyard and expects the ship to leave as intended tomorrow.' "

A ship couldn't be turned without it's rudder! To cut it off without being seen or heard, even at night, men would have had to cut it off below the water. Beth shivered, remembering how black and cold the water looked last night while they were out on the bay. She wouldn't have wanted to swim under water at night!

Her heart skipped a beat. She had seen someone swimming in the bay. She glanced at Will. He'd stopped reading and was staring wide-eyed at the newspaper.

He looked at her over the top of the paper. Was he thinking the same thing she was, that the men they'd seen in the other boat last night had cut the rudder?

Her heart started beating so loudly in her ears that she could hardly hear anything else.

"Nasty business," Josiah was saying.

Tim, seated on a stool before the hearth, glared at him. "If you mean it's rather a nasty business for Mr. Belcher to ship wheat and bread to other colonies when his neighbors are hungry, I agree with you, sir."

Beth stared at him, unable to believe her ears. It was unthinkable for a mere cabinetmaker's apprentice to dare to speak to a gentleman in such a bold manner!

"Tim." Mr. Smith spoke the one word quietly, but Beth heard the threat beneath it, as Tim must have also.

Josiah's face had grown red, and Beth could tell he was trying hard to keep his temper. Mary's face was red also. Was she embarrassed that Thomas had spoken to her suitor so unpolitely?

Josiah set his mug of cider on the table beside him, propped his hands on his thighs, and answered in a cold tone, "I sympathize with the people who are without flour or corn for bread, but I sympathize also with Mr. Belcher. His property was destroyed."

Beth remembered Tim saying Josiah's father and Mr. Belcher were friends. Of course he would defend the man.

"Josiah," Mary said somewhat timidly, "could Mr. Belcher not have sold the grain to the town, and the town sold it to the poor? I heard there are six thousand bushels of wheat on the ship, plus a great store of bread. That would feed many hungry people."

"He chooses to sell the wheat and bread elsewhere." Josiah turned his serious face to her. "You are right, Mrs. Allerton. The food he is sending away could do a great deal of good here in Boston. But that doesn't justify people destroying his property."

Tim jumped up, clenching his fists at his sides. His freckles stood out clearly on his angry face. "You believe, sir, that the lure of more money justifies Mr. Belcher sending away food when his neighbors' stomachs are hurting from hunger? They haven't asked for free food. The people of Boston are willing to pay for it."

Mrs. Smith gasped at Tim's statement.

Mr. Smith stood. "Timothy, you know better than to speak to your elders in such a disrespectful manner. Apologize to Mr. Foy, and then go to your room."

The fire crackling behind Tim was the only sound in the room. His chest heaved from his heavy, angry breaths. He opened his fists and closed them again. "I apologize, sir, for speaking out of turn."

Josiah nodded his be-wigged head in acceptance of Tim's apology, and Beth breathed a sigh of relief.

"But I won't apologize for what I think!"

"Timothy!" Mrs. Smith cried, both hands at her chest. Beth

knew she was embarrassed that a member of their household would speak to a guest that way. Children weren't to speak to adults at all unless spoken to, and never were they to speak disrespectfully.

"That is quite enough, Tim." Mr. Smith's lips were almost white. "We'll discuss your behavior tomorrow. Good night."

Tim stalked across the room toward the hall and stairway that led to the bedchambers.

He was barely out the door when Mrs. Smith apologized to Josiah. "I cannot imagine what he was thinking to speak in such a manner. Truly, I have never seen him behave that way to a guest before."

Beth hadn't either, but Tim always spoke meanly to her. Still, she rather admired the way he defended their poor neighbors.

Who was right? she wondered. Tim and the men who had sawed off the rudder, or Mr. Foy in defending Mr. Belcher? It seemed to her that both sides were partly right and partly wrong.

Were the men they saw last night the ones who cut the rudder?

Why had Tim wanted to go out on the bay at night, anyway? Yesterday he had spoken angrily of Mr. Belcher, and had said, "One of his ships, loaded with wheat and bread, is set to leave port tomorrow. Don't be surprised if it doesn't."

Had he known the rudder was to be cut? Had he gone out in the boat to help the men in some way? He'd brought a lantern along, and it appeared men at the next pier had signaled someone with a lantern. "It's time," he had said. Had he been a lookout?

Did Tim know who cut the rudder?

CHAPTER SIX
Trouble Breaks Out

Beth hurried through her morning chores and getting ready for breakfast. She wished she'd had a few minutes alone with Will last night to ask him what he thought about the men they saw on the bay and whether he thought Tim was involved in the rudder cutting.

She'd lain awake a long time last night wondering about it all. It was the first thing she thought of when the five-o'clock church bells woke her.

Now Will and Tim were fetching fresh water, so she still hadn't been able to talk to them.

When the table was set with the usual pewter and wooden mugs and plates, and a large brown pottery pitcher of milk had been brought in, she placed the bread on the table. The bread seemed more special to her after the events of the last two days.

And still Will and Tim weren't back.

Her father sat by the hearth reading the Bible as usual while they waited for the boys to return. Beth tried to keep Robert busy, but all he wanted was to get to the milk and bread.

Finally she heard the back door and the thunk of the water buckets being placed on the kitchen floor. Her father, mother, and Charles all stood and started to move toward the table.

Before they made it, Will burst into the room. He was panting, like he'd been running, and his clothes were covered with water that had sloshed over him from the buckets.

"Father," he gasped between breaths, "someone needs to stop them."

"Stop whom?"

Will waved in the direction of the pump and tried to catch his breath. "The men. There's a bunch of men, maybe fifty of them. They're angry about Mr. Belcher sending the grain away. They plan to force his ship to a wharf and keep it from sailing today."

Beth's jaw dropped. More trouble! It was hard for her to imagine Boston's citizens acting like this, like a mob.

"Where is Tim?" her father asked. "Didn't he come back with you, Will?"

Will shook his head. "He stayed to hear what the men were saying."

Mr. Smith started for the door. "Come, Charles. Perhaps there's a chance we can talk some sense into the men." Will started to follow them. Mr. Smith shook his head. "You stay here. No telling what trouble might take place when a lot of angry men get together."

Beth could understand why her father wanted Charles with him. Charles had a pleasant nature and an even temper. Everyone liked Charles. Maybe some of the younger men would know Charles and listen to him. He was a lot like her father, she realized.

It felt strange with only herself, Will, Mary, Robert, and their mother at the breakfast table. Even though there was only the five of them, Mother insisted Beth read the daily Bible selection when they were through eating. It was hard to concentrate on the words. She kept listening for the men to return.

Mother led the prayer after the Bible reading. A twinge of fear wriggled through Beth's chest when her mother prayed, "Keep our father and husband safe, Lord. Give him words of wisdom to speak to these men, and give the men ears willing to hear."

They still hadn't returned when the prayer was over and her mother told her to take the cow to the common to graze for the day. "Mind, if you see any groups of angry men, you come directly home. It appears the shenanigans of cutting Mr. Belcher's rudder the other night has excited a hornet's nest of excitement in this town."

Beth knew the men Will had seen were in the opposite direction from the common. Was her mother afraid there might be more angry groups about? She shivered at the thought, then set her lips firmly as she headed out to the back yard to get Millie.

Beth had just tied the rope around Millie's thick neck when Will stepped up beside her. "I've wanted a chance to talk with you. I've been thinking about the men we saw in the small boat that night on the harbor."

Beth nodded. "Me, too. Do you think they're the men who cut the rudder?" Her heart beat faster just thinking about it.

"I think so. I. . .I think Tim may know who they were, but he hasn't told me."

"I thought he might know," Beth agreed. She hesitated, trying to get up courage to ask the next question. "Do you think we should say anything to Father?" She wasn't sure she was brave enough to do that.

"He'd be furious with us for being out at night, especially on the harbor. It was a pretty stupid thing to do."

"I guess." *But it had been fun,* she thought.

Millie bumped Beth's chest with her huge nose. "Mooo!"

Beth rubbed the cow's soft nose to keep it from bumping her again. "Just a minute, Millie. The grass will still be there when we get to the common." She looked at Will. "Well, do you think we should tell Father?"

"We probably should, but he'd punish us good. And we don't know that the men in the boat were the ones who cut the rudder. Besides, even if they're guilty, we can't identify them."

Beth grinned, glad for an excuse not to get in trouble with Father. "You're right. We couldn't be any help at all."

Will stuffed his hands into the pockets of his leather breeches and kicked at a stone with his shoe. "I guess I thought telling Father about the angry men meeting this morning would make up for not telling him about the other night."

"Maybe it does."

Beth always liked taking Millie to the common. It was a chance to see other people and see what was going on about the town. But she tried to avoid the almshouse, where the town's poorest people lived on the edge of the common.

On the way back, she always tried to pass through the area of town that had been burnt by the Great Fire that still haunted her dreams. She especially liked seeing the new buildings that were going up to replace those that were burned. Over one hundred families had lost their homes in the fire, and many people like her father had lost their businesses. Most of the buildings that had burned were wooden. Some had been there since the town's beginning almost one hundred years before, and they had looked it.

Many of the new buildings were brick-tall, with flat roofs. All the new buildings were supposed to be brick so they wouldn't burn as easily, but not everyone could afford brick.

She glanced up at the front of the new town house as she stood in the middle of the largest street in Boston. It was here the selectmen met, laws were made for Massachusetts and Boston, people came to vote, and court was held. She thought the building was beautiful, with its tall brick walls and pillars that went all the way from the roof to the ground. The town house that burned had only pillars for the bottom floor.

First Church was just as impressive. It was three stories of brick, with a clock and a belfry. Soon it would hold its first service. The church even had an organ! She'd never heard one before.

She hurried along toward the bakery, where she was to pick up Samuel. Beth could smell the bakery before she arrived at it. The wonderful yeasty odor of baking bread filled the narrow street the bakery was built upon. A sheaf of yellow wheat painted on the sign over the door told people that this was a bakery, in case they couldn't tell from the mouth-watering aromas issuing from it!

The door entered into a wide hallway that ran all the way to the back of the building. On her left was the room where the bakery items were sold. On her right was the room where the breads, cakes, and other baked goods were made. She spotted Martha in that room right away.

Martha was wearing an apron that covered most of her work dress, but flour covered all of the apron and most of Martha. She was mixing bread dough in a waist-high wooden trough that stood on wooden legs. The long wooden paddle she was using to mix the dough reminded Beth of the oars on the boat they'd used the other night.

Beth quickly shifted thoughts. She didn't like the questions the memory of that night brought back.

She could tell how hard Martha was working from the sweat on her brow and the white knuckles closed about the paddle. After seeing how hard Martha worked, doing home chores and watching Robert and Samuel didn't seem so bad to Beth.

It was bright in the room where Martha worked. The plastered walls were painted white and reflected the morning sunshine that shone brightly through the windows overlooking the crooked little street.

The room behind it wasn't bright. There were no windows in the room. A door in the back wall led to the wood shed, where it was handy for the baker to grab wood to stoke the bake oven fires. The brick oven itself took up all of one wall.

Beth watched fascinated as the baker pulled open the black iron oven door with a metal rod. The interior of the oven glowed and flickered with orange light from the hard chunks of wood left behind by the dying fire. Nothing could be baked until the fire burned down.

Beth watched Baker Ames shove a flat wooden paddle into the oven to retrieve the mounds of bread baking there. The handle on the paddle was almost as long as Baker Ames was tall, so he wouldn't burn himself putting baked goods in or taking them out.

Heat surged from the oven into the bakery, and Beth moved back to where Martha was working beside an open window. "Hello. Is Samuel ready?"

Martha looked up and grinned. "Oh, hello. I'm sure Samuel's about somewhere." She wiped the back of a flour-covered hand over her forehead, plastering the tendrils of pale red hair there to her skin, and leaving behind a swatch of white. "Thank you for agreeing to look out for him."

"Isn't that what friends are for?" Beth wasn't about to tell her how much she dreaded the idea of watching two boys every day. She could see Martha's day would be more difficult than her own.

Martha stuck the wide end of her paddle into the dough in the trough and leaned against the paddle's handle. "I was surprised to see Mr. Foy with Mary last night. Why didn't you tell me they're keeping company? Has he asked her to marry him?"

Beth laughed. "No. Last night was the first time they were together. He's asked her to have dinner with his family tomorrow night. She's very nervous about it."

"I would be, too. Mr. Foy's father has one of the nicest homes in Boston. Can you imagine having dinner there?" Martha sighed. "I wouldn't mind just being a servant there so I could see what the house looked like inside."

Beth wrinkled her nose. "A servant, indeed! I'd rather have a home like that of my own."

"Did Mary like Mr. Foy, then, that she's agreed to have dinner at his home?"

"She hasn't said. But he's the only man she's allowed to court her, and it's been two-and-a-half years since Rob died."

Martha dug her paddle beneath the dough. With a grunt, she tossed the dough to the large, flour-covered wooden table beside her.

Beth watched Martha pull off a large chunk of dough, form it into a ball, and then punch both fists into it. A moment later something grabbed Beth's legs from behind, almost knocking her into the dough trough. "Oof!"

"I got you, Bet'!" Samuel cried out.

She peeled his hands from her legs. "You certainly did."

He grinned up at her with that sweet, tiny-toothed grin children have when they're almost three. His red hair was a riot of sun-drenched curls that formed a halo around his skinny, freckled face.

It was nice to be greeted so enthusiastically. She almost forgot that she had been dreading watching over him.

"Are we gain' to see Rob, Bet'?"

"Yes, in a minute."

"Good. I like Rob."

Beth slid her hands over his shoulders and pulled his back against her apron to keep him still. "Martha, did you hear about Mr. Belcher's rudder being cut?"

Before Martha could answer, the tinkle of bells sounded as the front door opened for a customer. A moment later Reverend

Cotton Mather stood smiling in the doorway.

"Oh, good morning, sir!" Martha greeted him. "Baker and Mrs. Ames are busy with the oven, but one of them will be with you in a moment."

"Reveren' Mat'er!" Samuel tugged away from Beth and threw himself across the room and against Cotton Mather's legs with the same exuberance with which he'd greeted Beth.

Cotton Mather chuckled so hard the waves of his white wig bounced on his wide shoulders. His chin was almost lost in his chubby neck as he looked down at the boy. "Hello, there, Master Samuel. How are you today?"

Sam gave him his babyish grin. "Fine. How are you?"

"Fine, thank you." He looked up at Martha. "How is your mother doing, Miss Martha?"

Martha's narrow face sobered. "She's worse, sir. She's too weak to work much and is resting."

"I'll just check on her and see if I can be of help." He peeled Sam's arms away from him as Beth had done. Digging into one huge pocket on his sensible black coat, he pulled out a penny and held it out to Samuel. "If you can say a Bible verse for me today, this penny shall be yours."

Sam didn't even hesitate. " 'For God so loved the world, that he gave his only begotten Son, that whosoever believeth in him should not perish, but have everlasting life.' John 3:16." He held out his little palm.

The reverend dropped the penny into it. "Very good, Samuel."

Reverend Mather hurried down the hall to the back room where Martha, Samuel, and Mrs. Lankford lived.

"He always has some little thing in his pockets for the small children," Martha said, punching away at the bread dough. "And he always has the children recite a bit of Bible or catechism when he gives them the gifts. He says children shouldn't learn that you receive something for nothing." She covered the dough with a damp cloth and set it to rise. "Now, what were you saying about Mr. Belcher?"

Beth told her about the rudder and about her adventure on the harbor at night and her and Will's suspicions. "And this morning, Will came on a mob of men, intent on preventing the ship from sailing now that the rudder has been replaced."

"What mob of men?"

Beth whirled about, surprised the reverend was back so quickly. She told him what Will had said, and how her father and Charles had hurried off to try calm the men. "Hadn't you heard of the meeting, sir?"

His eyebrows met in a concerned frown. "No. I shall proceed there immediately and see if I can be of help in stopping this mischief. The men of the town must see there is no wisdom in acting illegally."

He turned to leave, then turned about again. "I prayed for your mother, Miss Martha, but I'm quite concerned for her. Has she seen a doctor?"

"No, sir. She's taken some herb tea, is all."

"I think she must see a doctor."

Martha's face reddened. "I. . .we haven't much money, sir."

"I shall speak with a doctor myself, and see that he is paid."

"I. . .thank you, sir," Martha mumbled.

"I must see about that mob." He hurried out.

Baker Ames came into the room from the oven room. He was so sweaty that the shirt beneath his apron stuck to him. His long, thin gray hair was pulled back and tied with a string of leather.

He was scowling—just like usual, Beth thought.

He towered over slender little Martha. "What are ya doin', chatterin' the day away? There's work ta be done."

"I'm sorry, sir," Beth said, grabbing Sam's hand. "It's my fault. I stopped to pick up Samuel and started talking to her."

"Well, see that ya be gettin' along. I don't pay the girl ta gab."

"Yes, sir." Beth hurried out of the bakery with Samuel. *The awful man didn't pay Martha at all,* she thought indignantly, *unless you counted the food he gave her and the room he let her sleep in with her mother and brother. How could Martha and her mother stand it, working and living at the bakery?*

The spring morning air felt especially good after being in the hot bakery. Poor Martha, to be cooped up in that heat all day long!

Beth and Samuel didn't hurry home. She glanced in the windows and open doors of a tailor, a hat maker, a wig maker, and a tobacco shop that smelled strongly like the long pipes that so many men liked to smoke. They passed the printing shop where the colonies' only newspaper, the *Boston News Letter,* was printed each week.

Remembering her mother's orders, she and Samuel stopped at Mr. Franklin's candle shop. She always liked going to the candle shop. The smells were wonderful.

Mr. Franklin stood behind the table where he served his customers. "What can I do for you this fine day, Miss Beth?"

"A dozen bayberry candles, please."

"Ah, bayberry. A very good choice. They give the most pleasant odor when snuffed out. Ben, bring Miss Beth a dozen bayberry candles."

Beth watched the seven-year-old boy gather the candles and

then roll them in a piece of paper on the table before her, so she could carry them easily. Seeing him reminded her of the Great Fire. She'd seen Ben and his family in the streets that night. Their home and candle shop had been destroyed by the fire, like her father's shop. Ben had told her once how he'd had to climb out his bedchamber window to get away from the flames, the same as Martha's family.

Mr. Franklin leaned his elbows on the table while Ben wrapped the candles and said, "I hear your father did a masterful job of turning the tide of a mob's anger this morning, Miss Beth."

She stared at him in surprise. "He did?"

"Haven't you heard? My last customer told us about it. An angry group of men wanted to force the ship with Mr. Belcher's grain on it to shore."

"Yes, I know. But I haven't seen Father since he left the house."

"Well, according to my customer, he and that apprentice of his, Charles, did a fine job of convincing those men it wasn't smart to be doing something so illegal. Told them that they'd just bring down the anger of the law upon themselves if they did so, and that wouldn't feed anyone. The town's mighty beholden to your father, miss."

Pride filled her chest, leaving her feeling a bit embarrassed but very pleased.

After she had paid for the candles and was about to leave, Mr. Franklin said, "Tell your father I could use a couple more of his candle boxes. My customers like them."

"Yes, sir."

Life was strange, she thought. Two years ago Boston was fighting a war and a fire. Now the war was almost over, people were rebuilding their lives after the fire, but they had hunger to fight.

This time they were fighting among themselves: rich merchants like Mr. Belcher and the hungry people who couldn't afford bread.

At least Martha and her family, working at the bakery, had enough bread to eat.

CHAPTER SEVEN

Peace at Last

Beth didn't have much time the next few days to wonder about the conflict between Mr. Belcher and the townspeople. She was too busy trying to get her chores done while keeping Robert and Samuel in line.

Saturday she plucked the geese for feathers to refill the mattresses, a chore that had to be done every spring and fall. Gray goose down covered the old work dress she wore as well as the area around her. She sat on the low back step and looked out over the back yard. Where had the boys gone to now?

A wiggle in the mattress cover showed her. "Robert, Samuel, get out of that mattress ticking!"

All she heard was their giggles. The ticking bulged and jumped from the two boys inside it.

She grabbed a handful of down feathers from the goose in her arms. The goose struggled to get free. "I'm not hurting you," she scolded the bird. "It will be over sooner if you stay still."

The goose wasn't about to cooperate. It didn't like its feathers being yanked out any more than Beth liked to yank them out.

"Boys, get out of the mattress," Beth tried again in her sternest voice.

It did no good. The boys had learned quickly that when she had a goose in her arms, she couldn't chase them. She'd tried it a few times, and the goose had always escaped. A good thing she had the goose's head covered with an old stocking while she worked or she knew she would have been nipped many times.

Things had gone easier when her mother was helping. Now her mother was at the market getting fresh meat. Her mother wouldn't be much help to Beth the rest of day, either. Since it was Saturday, there was twice the usual amount of cooking to be done. Sunday was a day of rest, so no one in the family cooked.

Beth yanked another bit of down from the frustrated goose. "There, that's the last of it." She removed the stocking and freed the goose. It raced across the yard toward the other geese, honking its tale of hurt pride to whoever would listen.

Beth tucked a stray curl beneath the square cloth she'd tied over her head to keep the down out of her hair. Crossing to the mattress ticking that was half filled with feathers and boys, she opened it and peered inside. "Come out, boys."

They crawled out on all fours, still giggling. Feathers stuck to their breeches, shirts, faces, and hair. When they saw each other in the sunlight, they giggled all the harder, holding their stomachs and falling to the ground.

Beth couldn't help but laugh with them. They did look funny.

"If you had any more feathers on you, I'd mistake you both for geese!" She shook her head at them, trying to control her smile. "How am I ever going to fill up the mattress ticking if you two continue to mash down the feathers? Brush yourselves off, now, and quiet down."

The giggling only increased as they tried to brush each other off. Feathers drifted through the air. The boys soon forgot the brushing and chased the floating feathers.

Robert tried catching one of the floating feathers in his teeth, which promptly sent Samuel into another fit of giggles.

Beth gave up and went to catch another goose. The geese had learned to watch out for her this morning. No matter how calmly she approached them, they scurried out of her way, twisting their long necks to peck at her feet and honking their disapproval.

"Here, Goosey! Here, Goosey!" The boys ran into the gaggle of geese as fast as their little legs would carry them, waving their arms. The geese scattered further, protesting.

"Honk! Honk!" the boys tried imitating the geese.

The geese fled, their necks stretched out, large wings flapping. If their wings hadn't been clipped, Beth knew every one of them would have flown away.

She dropped to the ground, hooked her elbows around her

knees, and stared helplessly at the boys and geese running about the yard. "It's hopeless," she muttered.

How could she possibly keep them away from the geese and feathers while she worked? At this rate, she would never find time to work with the boys on their alphabet, and her father insisted she do so every day.

She sat up straighter. The alphabet! She hurried across the yard and finally managed to catch Robert's arm. "Why don't you and Samuel get your hornbooks and bring them outside?"

The boys cheerfully did as she asked. In a couple minutes they came out the back door, each grasping the handle of a wooden hornbook.

By this time Beth was again seated on the back stoop and had another goose in hand. "Sit on the ground by me and read the top line of your ABC's," she ordered. "Don't forget to point to the letters while you read."

The boys did as she said, crossing their legs and holding the hornbooks in front of them by the short handles, Robert's dark hair close beside Samuel's reddish-gold curls.

Robert's hornbook was the same one Beth and Will and Mary had used to learn their ABC's, and it was just like all the other hornbooks Beth had ever seen. It was shaped like a wooden paddle and only five inches tall and two inches wide. A thin, clear layer of horn covered the paper tacked to the board.

The first two lines of the paper listed the alphabet in small letters, the next two lines listed it in capital letters. Following that was a line of vowels. Next came three lines of simple sounds, like ab, eb, and ib. The Lord's Prayer took up the last half of the page.

The boys did well with the first half of the alphabet. Robert knew his letters better than Samuel, though Samuel was a few months older. Beth suspected Martha and her mother hadn't had much time to spend teaching Sam to read.

The rest of the morning went well, with the boys acting up only a couple more times. Still, Beth was glad when it was time for lunch, and she could have a break from watching them and plucking ornery geese.

Since it was Saturday, her father closed his shop early, like most of the businessmen. They believed the day of rest began at dusk on Saturday, rather than on Sunday morning.

Martha stopped early to pick up Samuel, too, as even grumpy Baker Ames closed early. Beth was sorry to hear her mother wasn't improving, in spite of the doctor which Reverend Mather had paid to visit her.

After Martha and Samuel left, Beth and her mother carried the mattress ticking inside, where Beth would stitch it shut again. But for now it sat in a corner of the kitchen out of the way. Beth smiled, thinking how plump and comfortable the mattress would be with all the fresh feathers.

While her mother and Mary prepared dinner, Beth heated water and bathed Robert near the kitchen hearth. He was a mess after rolling about in the feathers and dirt that morning! It wouldn't do for him to be so filthy for church the next day.

Mary chatted about Josiah Foy while they worked, telling Beth and her mother about his grand house with its fine furniture and beautiful china.

"The house sounds lovely," Mrs. Smith said, "but do you enjoy Mr. Foy's company?"

Mary bent her head over the carrots she was chopping, and her long blonde curls slid over her shoulders to hide her cheeks. "Yes," she said softly. "I believe I do."

Beth tried to think what it would be like if Mary married solemn, rich Mr. Foy, who was so different from little Robert's friendly, cheerful father. She couldn't imagine it.

Later when she and Mary were looking over their Sunday dresses to be sure they were ready for church, she asked Mary, "If you marry Mr. Foy, will you have many beautiful dresses?"

Mary looked flustered. "He hasn't asked me to marry him."

"But if he does, will you?"

"Will I what?"

"Have many beautiful dresses."

Mary lowered herself to the edge of the bed, holding her Sunday dress. "I suppose I would have some."

"He's awfully rich, isn't he?"

"Not awfully. His father is wealthy. He does own Foy Shipping Lines, after all. But he's lost a great deal of money during Queen Anne's War. A number of his ships were captured by pirates."

"But you told us of his fine house," Beth persisted.

"Yes, compared to us, he is very rich. I cannot imagine why Josiah has chosen to court me."

Beth knew what she meant. Wealthy young men in Boston almost always married women from wealthy families. Her gaze wandered over Mary's face with its petite nose, pointed chin, and blue eyes. Her blonde hair curled perfectly in a manner Beth could never manage with her own fly-away curls. In addition to her beauty, Mary had a sweet, generous spirit. "I can understand why he would like you," Beth said.

Mary smiled. "He hasn't expressed fondness for me yet. Now, let's check your gown and see whether it needs mending before tomorrow."

Beth held up the washed-out blue gown. "It doesn't need

mending, but it's too short, and the ribbons look as though I'd used them to tie the geese's beaks shut today."

Mary's laugh rippled out. "They aren't quite that bad." She lifted one of the limp ribbons on the elbow-length sleeve with a slender finger. "Perhaps this week we can find time to freshen them. We could use the pretty blue paper from the sugar loaf to dye them. Wouldn't that be nice?"

"Yes." The paper used to wrap the sugar loaves always gave the loveliest shade of blue. But Beth couldn't help wishing she had an entirely new gown to wear instead of having to be satisfied with freshly dyed ribbons to look forward to.

A gown like Josiah's sister's. She'd kept the drawing she'd made of the dress the day Miss Alice and Mr. Foy came to the house. Would her own father ever have enough money that she could have a gown made like that?

When dinner was over and the family gathered about the hearth, Beth was surprised that her father didn't immediately pick up the Bible for his usual Saturday reading.

"Wonderful news reached Boston today," he said, smiling on all of them. "The Treaty of Utrecht has been signed, ending Queen Anne's War."

Stunned silence filled the room.

"The war's truly over?" Beth asked.

"Yes, thanks be to God."

The boys, Mary, and Mother began to laugh. Will clapped Thomas on the back. "It's over!" Mary and Mother hugged. Charles lifted Robert and swung him around. "It's over, little man!"

Beth could hardly take it in. She lowered herself to a straight-backed, rush-seated chair by the hearth. "It seems so strange. I can't remember when we weren't at war."

Will grinned. "Of course you can't, silly. You were only a year old when the war started."

"You were only three when it started yourself." Beth shot back. "I knew Queen Anne ordered a cease-fire months ago, but there's been a little fighting since. I didn't believe there could be peace after all these years."

Massachusetts had paid dearly for the war, more than any of the other colonies, both in money and in lives. Beth had heard many times that taxes were four times higher than when the war started. It took a lot of money to pay soldiers and supply them with guns and ammunition and food. The taxes also helped the widows and children of those killed in the war, those who couldn't support themselves like Martha's mother or hadn't family to live with like Mary and Robert and had to live at the almshouse.

"Let's pray," Father said, "and thank God for peace."

Everyone bowed their heads and clasped their hands. "Thank Thee, Lord, that in Thy kindness, Thou hast given us the blessing of peace. We lift our hearts in gratitude that, on both sides, men will no longer be called to fight and die, that children won't lose their fathers, wives won't lose their husbands, and parents won't lose their sons to war. Help us to always remember the pain war causes, so we will always seek peace instead of war. In Jesus' name, amen."

"A—men!" Little Robert added.

Everyone laughed at his sincere but emphatic amen. But Beth noticed there were tears in Mary's eyes as she took Robert from Charles's arms and hugged him close, and she knew Mary was remembering her husband.

Father cleared his throat. "I hope this peace treaty means none of you boys ever have to fight. Not you, Will, or Charles, or Tim, or little Robert."

With one hand, Will smoothed Robert's thick brown hair. "I remember when Rob told me he'd volunteered to fight in the war. He said he wanted to do all he could to end the war, in the hope his children would never experience it. He would have been glad to know of the peace treaty."

Rob had never seen little Robert, Beth recalled. His son was born three months after he died.

So many young men from Massachusetts had lost their lives because of the war. Robert died in the battle for Port Royal, Nova Scotia. It was renamed Annapolis Royal, for Queen Anne, after the English and colonists won the battle with the French. After the battle, many colonial soldiers were ordered to stay at Annapolis. Less than one in five of them were still alive. Martha and Samuel Lankford and little Robert were only a few of the many Boston children whose fathers died because of the war.

The thought made Beth grateful for her own father. So many children lived with only their mothers or with their mothers and stepfathers. Beth had never known what it was like to lose one of her parents, and she hoped she never found out.

A year after Rob died, the British and colonists had prepared for another battle on the St. Lawrence. Some of the ships had smashed against the rocks of the great river, and eight hundred British soldiers drowned. The battle had been abandoned.

The Great Fire had happened less than a month later.

"Father," Beth said hesitantly, "Do you think God was punishing us with the war and the fire?"

"Why do you ask?"

Everyone stopped talking to listen. Her cheeks felt hot from the attention, but she continued anyway.

"Reverend Increase Mather said he thought God allowed the soldiers to drown and the town to be burned because the towns-people worked on Sunday, helping the English and colonial soldiers prepare the fleet for battle." Her family had gone to church that day almost two years ago as usual, so she didn't know why they should be punished, even if it were true. "So I thought maybe God used the war to punish us for something."

"That is a very important question, Beth," Father said. "Sometimes God does punish us when we don't try to follow His commandments, the same as people are punished by the court when they break a law."

"Like cutting the rudder on Mr. Belcher's ship," Will suggested.

"Yes," Mr. Smith said. "Of course, the trial for the rudder cutting hasn't been held yet. It's scheduled for Monday."

Beth's stomach turned over. If anyone found out she and Will and Tim had been on the harbor that night, would they be called to testify? The very thought made her feel sea sick.

"But back to your question, Beth," her father was continuing, "I don't know whether God was punishing us. I do know that we are to keep His commandments. Do you know what the most important commandments are?"

Beth hesitated. "The ones in the Bible verses we memorized?"

"Yes. Do you remember them?"

" 'Thou shalt love the Lord thy God with all thy heart, and with all thy soul, and with all thy mind. This is the first and great commandment. And the second is like unto it, Thou shalt love thy neighbor as thyself. ' "

Father leaned forward, elbows on the knees of his breeches. "You see, what we must learn from the war and the fire is that our buildings and the fine things we can no longer afford are not the most important things in life. Nothing can separate us from God's love. That's important. We have each other. That's important. Showing each other God's love in our daily actions is important. Would you agree?"

Beth glanced at Robert, sitting on Mary's lap. Sadness made her chest ache, knowing that Rob and Robert would never see each other on this earth. Her father was right. It was important to be kind to each other while we could. "I agree."

But she still missed the beautiful furniture they used to have, the nice clothes she used to wear, and the time she had to herself before she had to watch Robert and Samuel. And she didn't like the selfish way wanting these things made her feel.

Chapter Eight
The Trial

"I can hardly believe Father let us come," Beth whispered to Will, who was seated beside her in the large court room at the grand new town house.

Will's eyes danced with excitement. "I didn't think he'd let us come, either."

"I couldn't think of a thing to say when he asked us why we were so interested in this case. How smart of you to tell him it would be good for us to see for ourselves how the law works!"

Tim was seated on the other side of Will, and their father on the other side of Tim. Now Father leaned forward and shook his head at her. "Shhh."

She hadn't been speaking loud enough for him to hear what she'd said, she knew, but she was embarrassed just the same. At first she didn't think her father was going to let Tim join them. When Tim had asked to come, her father'd said he was needed at the shop. But Tim reminded him that he had been at the assembly of men who wanted to keep Belcher's ship from leaving port, and so had been allowed to join them.

Beth gave her attention back to the judge and lawyers at the front of the room. They'd been busy talking among themselves for a moment, but the business of the court seemed to be about to get underway again.

Beth had to peek around heads to see what was happening most of the time. She and Will were seated near the back of the room, and it was crowded with people. Near the front she saw Josiah Foy and his father, and she remembered that Josiah's father was good friends with Mr. Belcher.

Beth smoothed the skirt of her blue dress, the one she usually kept for church. She straightened the bow at her elbow, wishing there'd been time to dye the ribbons before today.

It was exciting to be here, but she wished the court moved faster. They'd spent a good amount of time this morning arraigning a jury. A Mr. Cumby was selected foreman. If things kept going this slowly, she'd be sent home to care for the boys. It had been kind of her mother to agree to watch them so she could come to court.

She was glad when the information about the rudder cutting was finally presented to the jury. Would anyone mention the small boat she and Will and Tim had seen with four men, two of whom had gone swimming in the middle of the night? She leaned forward anxiously during the testimony, her head tilted to look around the large white wig of the gentleman in front of her, her hands clenching her skirt.

No one mentioned the boat. When all the witnesses had been called, she leaned back, breathed a sigh of relief, and exchanged smiles with Will and Tim.

Mr. Cumby jumped to his feet, startling Beth. "Sure, and the men on the ship cut the rudder themselves!" he yelled. " 'Twas Mr. Belcher's men that did it, and not the good townspeople of Boston."

Mr. Belcher leaped up. "That is a bald-faced lie, sir!"

The judge pounded his gavel, but the spectators took up Mr. Cumby's chant. In a minute, they were all standing, and Beth and Will stood, too, to see what was happening. It took awhile for the court to quiet down. When it did, Mr. Cumby was dismissed as foreman, and another had to be selected.

She leaned close to Will to whisper in his ear. "Do you think we should tell what we saw that night?"

He whispered back, "It wouldn't help. We couldn't identify anyone, remember?"

His reminder made her feel better. She glanced down at her skirt. It was wrinkled where she'd clutched it in her sweaty hands. She clenched her hands together tightly in her lap so she wouldn't wrinkle her skirt more.

She shifted about. The whalebone hoop beneath her dress made it difficult to get comfortable.

Mr. Belcher and his attorney entered a bill, or charge, against the men who had gathered the morning after the rudder was cut, the men Beth's father and Charles persuaded not to force the ship to dock. The charge was read aloud, and then witnesses were called.

Father was one of the last called. Beth sat up straighter when he went forward, proud that he was part of this important trial.

The attorney asked him to tell what he knew in his own words. He told how Will had seen the group when he'd gone to fetch water, and how he and Charles had hurried there to try to convince the crowd not to harm Mr. Belcher's boat or interfere unlawfully with Mr. Belcher's business.

The attorney casually tucked a ruffle at his wrist into place. "Mr. Smith, were you able to determine which of the men were responsible for starting the gathering?"

"No, sir."

"And could you tell which of the men came up with the idea of forcing Mr. Belcher's ship to stay in harbor?"

"No, sir."

"Can you point to any specific men as leading the others?"

"No, sir."

"And have you any knowledge of who cut the rudder?"

"No, sir."

"What was the mood of the crowd when you arrived?"

"They were angry. They felt Mr. Belcher's grain was much needed in the town."

"Did you agree with their feelings?"

Mr. Smith hesitated. "I was not angry with Mr. Belcher. Even if I were angry, I don't believe an illegal act is acceptable, even to revenge an unkindness."

"Then why did you join the assembly?"

"To remind them that they are men whose honor is stronger

than their anger. Honorable men don't lower themselves to treat others or others' property in an illegal manner."

"And were you successful?"

"Yes, sir. The crowd broke up, and the men went their own ways."

Beth felt a swell of pride in her father. He'd stayed calm and answered all the questions put to him quietly and firmly. She remembered Mr. Franklin's words, that her father had done the town of Boston a great service.

Mr. Smith took his seat, and Charles was called. He answered everything quietly and verified everything Father had said.

Charles was walking back to his seat when Mr. Belcher leaped up. "I wish to be sworn in as a witness."

The room immediately hushed.

"Were you present at the assembly, Mr. Belcher?" the judge asked.

"No, but I've spoken with a number of men, and—"

"If you did not see the assembly first hand, you have nothing to say which can interest the court."

Mr. Belcher's heavy cheeks flushed. "Sir, these. . .these scoundrels have attempted to interfere with my livelihood."

"That is something for the court to decide."

"But, sir—"

The gavel banged. "Sit down, Mr. Belcher, and allow the court to proceed."

Mr. Belcher stared at him. Beth's heart raced. Would Mr. Belcher obey and sit down? He was so angry he was shaking. Even the lace ruffles poking out from the heavily embroidered coat cuffs quivered. "Sir—"

His attorney yanked at the sleeve of Mr. Belcher's expensive coat. The man finally sat down.

Beth noticed Josiah frowning in Mr. Belcher's direction. Did he think his father's friend's actions disgraceful?

The jury retired to a chamber to deliberate, and the spectators rose, stretched, and wandered about the room or out into the street to wait for their return.

They hadn't long to wait. The jury was soon back.

The spectators took their seats. They were so quiet that Beth could hear wooden wheels and horses' hooves in the street outside the open windows. Everyone's eyes were directed toward the jury foreman.

When asked for the verdict, the foreman stood. "We are unable to convict anyone. The evidence does not tell us who is responsible for cutting the rudder or encouraging the people to do Mr. Belcher's ship additional harm."

Cheers went up all about them—Tim's among them. Father clamped a hand on Tim's shoulder. Tim quit cheering, but Beth saw his grin didn't grow any smaller. She and Will exchanged uneasy glances.

"Quiet!" The judge's gavel banged again and again.

The crowd was just beginning to quiet when Mr. Belcher, on his fat, silk-stockinged legs once more, cried, "This is an outrage!"

A man with dirty gray hair and stubble on his chin, who was dressed in a worn brown coat, shook his fist. "It's you who is the outrage! 'Tis an ill act toward your neighbors to send away so great a quantity of wheat in this time of scarcity."

"I may sell my property to whom I please!"

The man in the brown coat stuck out his chin. "The Bible says, 'He that withholds corn, the people will curse him.' "

"The people might say all they will against me, but they may not harm my property, and it is wrong of the court not to say so!"

"The jury has spoken, and you'd be wise to listen to them," was the bold reply.

The crowd cheered again and began filing from the room, many laughing loudly at Belcher's discomfort.

"That will teach him!" Beth heard someone say.

Outside the building, Josiah Foy stopped to greet them. His green coat with its lapels and huge, turned-back cuffs decorated with brass buttons and embroidery looked especially fine beside Father's plain fawn-colored coat, but Josiah didn't act as though he noticed.

He clasped his hands behind his back. The frown beneath his wig gave him a worried look. "What do you think of the verdict, Mr. Smith?"

"Considering the mood of the crowd, I think it was a wise verdict. There may have been violence if the men who gathered the other morning were punished when they did nothing but grumble."

Josiah nodded, still frowning. "Yes, your point is well taken. But Mr. Belcher is very angry with the verdict. He believes his business interests are not being protected."

"The townspeople feel their food interests aren't being protected!" Tim declared belligerently.

"Timothy!" Father's voice was sharp.

Tim pressed his lips hard together and clenched his hands at his sides. Charles laid a hand on his shoulder and gave him a warning look.

Beth and Will exchanged shocked glances. Tim had lately taken to speaking out in a manner unacceptable for someone of his age and position. What was happening with him?

Mr. Foy had looked startled at Tim's outburst, but he only said, "The people may have won this battle, but according to Mr. Belcher, they will not win the bread war. He says as a result of this verdict he will send even more grain away, and what he sells in Boston will be sold at three times the present price."

Beth gasped. "Can he do that?"

"Can't the selectmen forbid it?" Will asked.

"We will have to see," Father answered.

Josiah met her father's gaze. "When this unhappy affair began, I believed the townspeople were wrong and Mr. Belcher was in the right. I still believe the townspeople's actions were illegal and ugly, but I am concerned with Mr. Belcher's anger. Should he follow through with his threat, he will not be acting honorably. If his neighbors need the grain, he should see they have it—and at a fair price." He sighed. "I fear my father's friend has forgotten the rest of the Bible verse the man inside quoted."

"What is it?" Beth asked.

"The verse is from Proverbs. It says, 'He that withholds corn, the people will curse him; but blessing shall be upon the head of him that sells it.' I'm afraid Mr. Belcher is missing a blessing."

"Perhaps Mr. Belcher will feel more kindly when he's allowed his anger to cool down," Father said.

Tim snorted.

Father darted his apprentice a sharp look. "We shall pray, and ask the Lord to give the selectmen wisdom in this matter, and provide bread for the people. There are still a couple months before the grain and corn is harvested."

"Yes," Josiah nodded. "Yes, we shall pray."

Beth looked from one to the other, and fear wriggled into her stomach. Were things as bad as they seemed from the men's faces? Would Mr. Belcher carry out his threat? She glanced at Will. He looked as worried as the men. What was happening to the peaceful, happy town of Boston?

CHAPTER NINE

To the Almshouse

"W-X-Y-Z," Robert and Samuel finished together, their pudgy fingers pointing proudly to the last of the letters on their hornbooks.

"Very good." Father beamed at them. "You'll soon be reading as well as Beth and Will."

The boys grinned at each other.

Happiness swelled through Beth. She knew her father's praise was directed as much at her as at the boys, for without her efforts, neither would yet know their alphabet. True, they still stumbled occasionally in the middle, but they were ready to go on to identifying the simple sounds listed below the alphabet on their hornbooks.

She'd resented working with them at first. It was so frustrating when they refused to pay attention! Robert could be quite stubborn about having his own way. She hadn't known it would feel so good when the boys mastered the alphabet.

Mary, sewing by the sitting room window, smiled. "I'm very proud of you, Robert. The entire alphabet!" Her blue-eyed gaze met Beth's. "Thank you. I'd never have had time to teach him his letters."

"You're welcome."

Mary's eyes twinkled. "Mother, have you told Beth of your surprise?"

"What surprise?" Beth swung toward her mother.

Mrs. Smith smiled. "Your father and I have decided it's time you had a new dress."

She bounced to her feet. "Truly?"

"Truly. Do you know what style you'd like?"

"Oh, yes! I want a dress like Miss Alice Foy's! I've a drawing of it."

She raced to her room, found her drawing, and raced back down. She could hardly believe it! After all the long months of hoping! "Thank Thee, Lord," she whispered.

She'd just handed the drawing to her mother when there was a knock on the door. Martha had come to pick up Samuel. Beth could see she'd removed her bakery apron and tried to brush the flour from her thin gown, but there were still traces of her day's work about her. Her narrow shoulders drooped, and there were grayish-blue circles beneath her green eyes.

Guilt flooded through Beth. Caring for the boys wasn't much of a struggle compared to Martha's work.

Samuel raced across the room, threw his arms around Martha's legs, and grinned up at her. "I can say my ABC's!"

Both boys had to show her their newest ability. They did so at the top of their lungs, to the amusement of everyone in the room.

William and Tim looked up from the goose quills they were scraping and cutting for pens. Her mother listened with a smile on her worn face. As she bent over Beth's sketch, her small white cap hid her bun of graying hair.

Mary's needle was idle, the material of the beautiful dress she was sewing lying over one end of the table where it wouldn't get dirty, while she watched the boys. Charles and Father smiled indulgently from the other end of the table where they were going over the customers' orders for the cabinetmaker's shop, planning the next few weeks' work, and figuring how much and what kinds of wood they would need.

Father used to work at his accounts at a fine secretary or desk, Beth remembered. It had been sold like so much of their furniture. He never complained of missing it. Did he miss it like she did, quietly but painfully, like something that burned inside her chest when she thought of it? Miss seeing its beautiful design against the wall and the way the grain of the wood had swirled so beautifully on the slant-board that opened to a desk?

Martha let the boys know she was properly impressed with their achievement and turned to greet the others. Robert and Samuel promptly sat down on the floor and began chanting the

91

alphabet to each other.

Beth was glad the boys were through so she could tell Martha about her new dress. She smiled broadly when Martha admired her sketch of the dress. "It will be lovely. Is that what Mary is working on?"

"No. She's working on a gown for a customer." Beth led her over to the table.

"Oh, Mary, what beautiful materials!" Martha stared down at the dress spread like an elegant cloth across the table.

Mary agreed. "The overskirt is a new style. It's to be pulled back more at the sides than is usual, to show off the ruffles on the underskirt. See?" She handed Martha a small doll-like figure which had been sent over from England dressed in the new fashion.

Martha examined the tiny dress eagerly. "It must be lovely, spending your days working with fine material and creating beautiful dresses."

"I admit I usually do enjoy it. But today I'm having trouble making the overskirt work right. I've looked and looked at the pattern doll, but I can't understand how they made the overskirt puff out in such a manner."

Martha turned back the doll's small overskirt to study the stitching. Then she reached for the gown Mary was sewing. She hesitated with her hand just above the material. "May I?"

"Certainly."

Beth let her gaze drift back to the boys, who were still showing off to each other. She loved beautiful gowns, but she wasn't in the least bit interested in how they were made.

She waited every day for Martha to come pick up Samuel. The only times they were able to see each other any more were when

Beth picked Samuel up in the morning and when Martha picked him up in the evening. She missed the days they used to sit beside each other in dame school and walk to and from school together, giggling and chattering like Samuel and Robert were now.

"I think I found the problem, Mary," she heard Martha say. "The gathers in this area need to be turned back slightly to make the material puff out, see? You have them turning toward the front of the gown."

Beth turned back and watched Mary study the area Martha had pointed out.

"Why, I believe you're right." Mary smiled at Martha.

"And if you stitch an inch upward along this point, the gathers won't be able to turn back."

"You certainly have an eye for sewing, Martha."

"She always has had," Beth said. "She was always showing me how to correct the stitching errors I made in dame school."

Mary bent to her work, her blonde curls sliding over her shoulder to catch in the small white ruffle along the wide collar of her calico gown.

There was a knock at the door, and Will went to answer it. Everyone was surprised when Josiah Foy came into the room with him.

Beth saw Mary's hand drop her needle and fly to her curls, and knew she wished she'd had time to freshen up. A lovely pink stole over Mary's cheeks, and her eyes lit up. *Was she growing especially fond of sober Mr. Foy?* Beth wondered.

Josiah bowed slightly toward Mr. Smith. "Please forgive me for barging in without asking leave to visit. I was returning home from dining with friends and thought I would enjoy a few minutes of your family's company."

More likely of Mary's company, Beth thought. She exchanged a quick glance with Martha, trying to hide her smile.

Father welcomed their guest warmly and invited him to sit in his chair.

"Thank you, but first, I've a gift for Beth."

Beth stared at him. Surely she hadn't heard right! But he crossed the room to her and pulled something out of one of his coat's huge pockets.

"Drawing talent such as yours deserves the best tools." He handed her an inkhorn of the finest leather.

A lump formed in her throat. She swallowed hard. "I never thought to have anything so wonderful. Thank you."

He smiled and joined her father near the hearth.

Mary and Martha both told her how lovely the inkhorn was. Then Mary glanced across the room where Josiah was seated and sighed. "I hate to be rude when he's come to visit, but I promised the dressmaker I'd finish stitching this part of the gown tonight."

"I'll do it," Martha offered.

"I couldn't ask such a thing of you."

"It will be a joy to work on such a beautiful gown."

Mary, after a moment's hesitation, thanked her and went to sit beside Josiah.

Robert, who surprisingly never seemed to be put off by Josiah's stern manner, hurried over to inform him that he had conquered the ABC's. Then nothing would do but that he and Samuel demonstrate their skill. Josiah even smiled slightly at the boys when they were done and told them how well they had recited.

It wasn't long before the conversation came around to Mr.

Belcher. "He is spoken against everywhere you go: taverns, streets, wharves, shops, the market. People are angrier with him than ever," Charles said.

Josiah sighed. "It's been two weeks since the trial. I'd hoped his anger would cool. It hasn't."

"Baker Ames is very angry with him," Martha said, somewhat timidly. "Mr. Belcher raised the cost of flour to three times what it was. Baker Ames had a hard time paying for his last purchase. Although the price of flour is higher, the selectmen haven't increased the price at which he can sell his bread."

Beth looked at Martha. Baker Ames was ornery enough in normal times. Martha had told her yesterday that he'd been even more difficult lately. She wished Martha and her mother didn't have to live and work there.

"Baker Ames is fortunate to be able to purchase flour at any price," Josiah said. "I suggested to one of the selectmen that they use town tax money to purchase grain and sell it to the town poor at pre-war prices. The selectmen tried. There was no grain to purchase. Belcher had bought it all up. And he refuses to sell to the selectmen."

Beth stared. "How can anyone be so mean!"

"Beth, don't be rude," her mother said quietly.

But Josiah just shook his head. "Hurt pride can make a man do many foolish things."

"Just like empty stomachs," Will said.

"Yes," Josiah agreed. "Hunger also makes people do things they wouldn't do otherwise. The talk against Mr. Belcher has the council so concerned that the selectmen have agreed to take turns walking Boston's streets at night to prevent mischief."

"Isn't that the constable's duty?" Will asked, looking up from

95

the goose quills he was bundling together.

"They're concerned the constables can't keep the peace by themselves, and the town hasn't enough money to hire more."

Mother began lighting the candles in the room, and Beth realized dusk was falling.

Martha rose. "I must be getting Samuel home."

Beth walked with them to the door. When the three of them reached the entryway, Martha whispered, "I didn't want to say anything in front of everyone, but I've been wanting to tell you all day. Baker Ames says with the price of flour so high and Mother still not well, Mother won't be able to work for him anymore. He says we'll have to leave."

"Leave!"

Martha nodded, glancing over Beth's shoulder to see whether anyone had heard her exclamation. "Mother's going to ask him to take me on as an apprentice."

"But you don't want to be a baker!"

"If I'm an apprentice, he and his wife will have to let me stay with them." She blinked back tears and smiled bravely. "Besides, if Mother can't afford to take care of me, the town will apprentice me to someone. Who knows where that might be? I might like the bakery better."

A lump came to Beth's throat, making her throat ache. "Where will your mother and Samuel go?"

"To the almshouse."

Chapter Ten
Will God Answer?

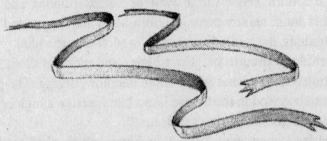

Beth sat on a stool in the doorway that led to the backyard. The door was open, as was the kitchen window, for it was a warm day, and there was a fire in the fireplace. From where she was seated, Beth could watch both the fireplace and boys, who played in the yard. A blue jay sat on the fence nearby, chattering loudly at the geese.

It had already been a long morning, and there must be another hour before noon. She sighed and went back to mending the hole in the toe of Will's long black stocking. She wished she were working on her new dress instead, but the material hadn't even been bought.

"Hi!"

She started at Charles's voice, poking the needle into her thumb. "Ouch!"

"Sorry." He looked into the three kettles hanging by chains from the huge bar at the top of the fireplace. "What's for lunch? Not goose quills, I hope!"

She grinned at his foolishness. The quills Will and Tom had trimmed the night before were boiling in one of the kettles. They had to be boiled until they were clear. "Lunch is cornmeal pudding sweetened with molasses." It too was being boiled, in a bag in another of the brass kettles. "And cherries with cream."

In the third kettle she'd dyed her dress ribbons and also another long, skinny piece of cloth Mary had suggested they stitch along the white line that showed where the hem on her church dress used to be. The ribbons and piece of cloth were hanging over branches in the apple tree now, drying. The piece of cloth bounced in the breeze like a banner from a high branch where the geese couldn't reach it.

Charles leaned against the door frame and brushed his long, straight brown hair behind his ears. "Looks like Robert and Samuel are behaving pretty well."

"For the moment. You should have seen them trying to help me weed the garden this morning. They wanted to pull up everything green, including the corn and beans."

He laughed, and she couldn't help but smile. "I guess it is funny now, but it wasn't at the time."

"It's good to see you smile again," he said. "You were looking mighty unhappy at the morning meal."

She hadn't thought anyone had noticed. She'd had that horrid dream again. It was because of Martha's awful news, she supposed. She bit her lip and concentrated on weaving the darning needle through the edge of the stocking hole.

"Would you like to tell me about it, Beth?"

She looked up at his kind brown eyes. If there was anyone who would understand how she felt, it would be Charles. She lowered her needle and took a deep breath. "It's Martha. Baker Ames is letting her mother go. Mrs. Lankford and Samuel have to move to the almshouse, and Mrs. Lankford has asked Baker Ames to apprentice Martha."

"Whew!" Charles slid his back down the wall until he squatted beside her, his elbows resting on the leather work apron covering his breeches. "No wonder you're upset. That's a lot for your friend Martha to go through." His gaze slid to the boys playing among the scattering of pale apple blossoms beneath the apple tree, and a frown cut between his eyebrows. "Hard for Samuel, too."

Was he thinking of when his parents died in London? But he hadn't been sent to an almshouse. He'd been sent to the Smiths' house instead.

He lay his large hand gently over hers. The callouses on his palms from his woodworking were rough against her skin. "You know, Beth, the almshouse isn't so awful. The town built it so people would have a place to go when they don't have a place of their own, a place they could live quiet, peaceful, and godly lives."

"But it's so crowded, what with all the war widows and people still without homes after the fire. Everyone says there are too many people there for the size house. And. . ." She gulped and raced on, telling him her worst fear. "And prisoners are kept there."

"The prisoners are kept in another part of the building. They wouldn't be allowed to hurt Sam or his mother."

Was he telling the truth? She searched his eyes. He looked calmly back at her. "Some of the children tell of awful things that happen there," she said.

"What kids? Kids who have lived there?"

"N. . .no. Just neighbors and kids at dame school."

"They only like to try frighten each other. It's a good place. The town has bought tools and spinning wheels so the people who go there have a way to make some money. Every Sunday a preacher goes there to speak in case the people can't make it to church. Now that doesn't sound so bad, does it?"

"No. But. . ." Beth struggled to find a way to put her worries into words. "It's not a home."

"Not like your home, no. Homes and families aren't all the same. Martha and Samuel's father isn't alive, but that doesn't mean they haven't had a home with their mother."

"In a dark little room in the back of Mr. Ames's bakery. You call that a home?"

He nodded. "They have each other. That makes it a home."

"Well, they won't have each other anymore. At least, Martha won't. Not if Baker Ames apprentices her. Then she'll live in that dark room alone."

"We're never all alone. Christ promises to be with us always, remember?"

She'd forgotten. "It's not quite the same, is it?"

"No. But He's there."

She picked at the sock in her lap. "When your parents died and you crossed the ocean on a ship, did you think about Christ being with you?"

"I sure did."

She glanced at him. He gave her one of his wonderful smiles. "Did it help?"

"Yes." He sighed and ran a hand through his shiny dark hair. "There are lots of children who lose their parents, Beth. There's many without their fathers in Boston now because of the war. It's unfortunate, but life is that way sometimes. That's why so many orphaned boys are sent to America to be apprentices, the way I was."

"But weren't you scared?" she burst out. "Not of the ocean, but of what you'd find here?"

"Of course. All of the boys on that ship were afraid. But the people of London were doing the best thing they could for us. They knew we had a better chance of learning a trade here in New England than in Old England. It's the same with the town of Boston. Poor children are apprenticed so they have a way to learn a trade and someone to see that they learn to read, have a place to stay, decent clothes to wear, and food to eat."

"What if they don't want to be apprenticed?"

He seemed to ignore her question to ask her one. "Do you know what I learned on that trip from London?"

She shook her head.

"I learned not to be afraid of the unknown. The unknown is just a place where new experiences wait for us. Do you know what was at the end of that trip for me?"

"Boston."

He grinned. "You're partly right. Boston was here. So was your father and his cabinetmaker's shop and his family. He's been a good master. He treats me and Tim more like sons than his apprentices. My apprenticeship will be over in less than a year. Thanks to your father's training, I'll be able to earn a good living with my skill."

He leaned forward and squeezed her hand. "Beth, it's usually a good thing for poor and orphaned children to be apprenticed out, even if it means separating the children from their families. It's one way God watches out for children. What would happen to them if no one saw to their education and training?"

"I guess you're right. But Martha doesn't want to be a baker. Even if she did, she wouldn't want to be apprenticed to grumpy old Baker Ames."

He pressed his lips together and nodded. "I don't know what the answer to that is, but God does. Why don't you pray for her?"

Her lips trembled when she smiled at him and nodded. She'd pray. Would God answer?

The door between the kitchen and sitting room—kept shut to keep the heat from the kitchen fireplace out of the rest of the house—was flung open, and her mother hurried in with her usual bustling manner.

"Why, child, haven't you finished mending that stocking yet? And Charles, what are you doing in my kitchen instead of the shop? Shoo, and let Beth and me get the meal on the table."

He gave Mrs. Smith his charming grin, winked at Beth, and ambled out of the kitchen.

It had been awfully nice of God to let Charles come all the way across the ocean to live with them, Beth thought.

Beth had a special treat that afternoon. Her mother took her along to purchase material for her new dress. Even trying to keep Robert and Sam from getting into trouble at the shop couldn't take away her excitement.

Joy seemed to bubble right up out of her toes and into her heart. She'd dreamed of having a new dress for so long. Now that it was real, she couldn't decide which material she wanted. She glanced longingly at the rich damasks and silks but knew they were too expensive, so she didn't even mention them to her mother.

One day, she promised herself, when she was a wealthy married woman, she'd come into this shop and buy whatever material she wished and not think about the price.

She finally settled on a print for the underskirt, which would show like a panel down the front of her dress, tiny red flowers against a white background. For the outerskirt she selected a sunny yellow. White cotton was purchased for the flounced sleeves and red ribbon to match the flowers for the sleeves and sash at the waist. This dress was sure to be as beautiful as Josiah's sister's gown!

But her excitement over the dress was forgotten that evening at dinner when her parents announced that Mary had agreed to wed Josiah.

CHAPTER ELEVEN
An Answer for Martha

Beth stared across the table at Mary, then glanced at Will. His mouth was hanging open, and she realized hers was too. She'd known Mary was fond of Josiah, but she hadn't expected her to promise to marry him yet.

Mary's cheeks grew red. "It's not unusually soon. Many people become engaged with less courting time."

"You knew Rob for seven years before you married him," Will protested.

Mary laughed. "Rob was Father's apprentice for seven years. He couldn't marry until his apprenticeship was over. Josiah is already a businessman. Besides, there's his son, Thomas, to think of. He's only a year old. Josiah feels it's important for Thomas to have a mother."

Robert screwed his round little face into a frown and looked up from his seat beside her. "Why is Thomas going to have a mother?"

"So he will be a happier little boy," Mary answered patiently.

"Oh. Why?"

"Because Josiah loves him and wants the best for him."

"Oh. Does Josiah love Rob?"

Mary hesitated, smoothing his long brown hair. "He likes Rob very much."

Robert smiled, satisfied, reached for his mug of milk, and let the adults go back to their conversation.

"Congratulations, Mary." Charles smiled at her. "I hope you'll be very happy."

"Thank you."

It was like Charles to be the first to say something nice to her about her engagement, Beth thought. *Why hadn't she thought to say something like that herself, right away?* "I hope you'll be happy, too, Mary."

"Me, too," Will said. "When will the wedding be?"

"In a month. The law says the banns have to be posted on the church door and announced in church for three weeks before we can marry."

Beth wondered what her father had promised to Josiah. A former apprentice like Rob might be satisfied with only his bride, but wealthy men always received dowries from the families of the women they married. What could her father afford to give to a man like Josiah in these times when money and other things were so scarce?

As if he'd heard her thoughts, her father grinned at Will. "You and Charles and Tim are going to be kept busy the next few months. We'll be making furniture for Mary to take to her new home: a dining table like this one, a cupboard for her dishes, six walnut chairs, and a secretary desk."

Beth gasped.

"All that?" Tim's eyes were huge beneath his mop of curly hair.

Her father just kept grinning. "All that."

Mary smiled at the boys. "I thank all of you in advance for the hard work you will be doing for me. I have no doubt the pieces will be among the finest in Boston."

Beth quickly lifted her pewter mug to her lips to hide her laugh as Will, Tim, and even Charles sat up a little straighter.

"There will be more work for you, too, Beth," her mother said.

Beth almost choked on her milk. "Me?"

"Yes. We'll have to make bridecakes for our friends, and Mary must have some new clothes before the wedding. Robert, too. Josiah will expect his family to dress well."

Beth groaned. More sewing! "What about my new dress?" Would she have to give the material to Mary? It was going to cost her father a lot of money to buy new clothes besides make the furniture. He would have to use some of the money he'd been trying so hard to save to build a new shop.

Mary placed a hand on Beth's arm. "We'll start your dress first."

"Mary!" her mother protested.

"She's waited so long," Mary said quickly. "We can cut her

dress out tonight, and Beth can begin working on it. Then we can sew together in the evenings. I'll work on my dresses and Robert's things, and that way I can help her if she has trouble." She smiled at Beth over Robert's head.

Beth smiled back. A warm feeling filled her chest. She was going to miss Mary after she was married.

The next two weeks the house and shop were busier than ever. Everyone knew the furniture wouldn't be ready in time for the wedding, but that didn't matter. It wasn't unusual for a dowry to be received months after the marriage took place. Beth's father said he wanted Josiah to see they were working on the furniture. Besides, he said, they'd never finish it if they didn't start it.

Beth spent every minute she could spare working on her dress. For the first time, she wished she'd applied herself to becoming a skillful seamstress, like Martha and Mary. She wanted her dress to be beautiful!

It wasn't easy to sew well and watch Robert, too. With her mother and Mary spending so much time making Mary and Robert's new clothes, Beth was more responsible for Robert than ever. She urged him through his horn book every day, listening to him call out the alphabet first, and then "a-b, ab! e-b, eb! i-b, ib!" until he'd gone through all the short syllables.

Some days he grew stubborn. Since Mrs. Lankford no longer worked at the bakery, she kept Sam with her all day. Robert missed his little friend. He didn't understand why his Sam didn't spend his days with him anymore. When he begged Beth to see him and couldn't, he simply refused to do as she asked. On those days, Beth thought she could hardly wait for him to move to Josiah's house!

Beth hardly saw Martha anymore. Sometimes she went to the

bakery in the evening on her way to the common to bring Millie home for the night. She and Martha were seldom able to visit. Martha often had to work at night mixing dough for breads so they would be ready to put in the oven first thing in the morning. Mrs. Ames always had something for her to help with if she was done in the bakery. When Martha had a few spare minutes, she'd go to the almshouse to visit her mother and Sam.

Martha always looked tired. She had big circles under her eyes from working long hours. One day Beth asked, "Has Baker Ames decided yet whether he'll apprentice you?"

"No." Martha bit her lip and stared at her shoe where her stocking showed through a hole. "Every day he says I'm too slow and small to be any use to him."

Beth boiled with anger at his cruel words. "I notice that hasn't kept him from working you sunup to sundown!"

Martha, like always, didn't complain. What could she do? There was no place else for her to go. "Maybe when harvest time comes and there's more grain available, he won't be so grumpy."

"I don't believe anything will ever make Baker Ames pleasant or fair to you."

At first Beth had been so excited about Mary's coming wedding that she'd told Martha all the fun details about the new clothes and furniture. Martha had smiled and acted interested, but finally Beth quit talking about it much. She felt guilty that things were going so nicely for her family when things were just going from bad to worse for Martha's family.

She'd followed Charles' advice and prayed for Martha every day, but she hadn't seen God answer her prayers. *Why was He so slow answering?* she wondered while she walked Millie home one night through Boston's crooked streets with the high, closely built buildings looking down on them. Wasn't He going to answer at all? Didn't He care about poor children like Martha and Sam?

She tried to forget Martha's problems while she worked on her dress. She didn't want anything to take away from the fun of having a new frock.

Mary was patient in helping her, and Beth tried hard to make the careful, tiny stitches that Mary suggested.

One evening when Mary was late returning from her job, Beth asked, "Are you going to keep working for the dressmaker Mrs. Brock after you're married?"

"Oh, no, Josiah would never permit his wife to have a position outside the home."

Beth took another stitch in the hem of her yellow overskirt and sighed. "I wish Martha could be apprenticed to someone nice like Mrs. Brock instead of to that mean Baker Ames." Hope beat in her chest. Why hadn't she thought of that before? "Do you think Mrs. Brock would apprentice Martha?"

Mary dropped the tucking she was working on to her lap and leaned forward eagerly. "What a wonderful idea! Martha certainly has a gift for sewing. I'll ask Mrs. Brock tomorrow if she will consider her. Even if she's interested, she'll have to meet Martha before she decides."

Beth started to her feet, but sat down quickly again when the beautiful yellow overskirt began to slip to the floor. She didn't want it dirty before she'd even worn it! "I wish I could tell Martha right now!"

"Oh, no! You mustn't get her hopes up until we know whether Mrs. Brock will see her."

It was awfully hard not to tell. Beth avoided the bakery on her way from the common, afraid she wouldn't be able to keep her secret. She could hardly wait for Mary to get home from Mrs. Brock's that evening. Every chance she got, she looked out the sitting-room window or front door and down the crooked lane in hopes of seeing Mary return.

When Mary finally did get home, Beth was setting the table. She let the pewter plate in her hands clatter to the table as soon as she saw her. "Did you remember to ask about Martha?"

Mary nodded, grabbing both of Beth's hands and grinning. "Mrs. Brock said she will see her tomorrow evening. I'll go with her, if you think that will make her more comfortable."

Beth threw her arms around Mary's neck in a happy hug. "Oh, Mary, you're wonderful!"

Beth had a hard time convincing her mother that she couldn't wait until after the evening meal to see Martha, but finally Mrs. Smith gave in and let her go to the bakery.

Beth helped Martha finish up the evening dishes. Sometimes she had to bite her lips to keep from telling her news, but she knew it wouldn't be wise to say anything where Baker Ames might overhear.

Finally Mrs. Ames excused Martha from further chores for the day. Beth grabbed Martha's hand and all but dragged her outside, hurrying down the street where she was sure Baker Ames and his wife wouldn't overhear them through an open door or window.

"Where are we going?" Martha asked, trying to keep up.

Beth didn't answer. She simply pulled her along until they reached a corner with no people walking by to hear her. Then she swung about so fast that Martha had to jerk to a stop to avoid bumping into her.

"Goodness, Beth, what's the hurry?" Martha laughed, trying to catch her breath.

"Would you like to be a seamstress?"

"What?"

"You don't want to be a baker, do you?"

"No."

"And Baker Ames hasn't signed your apprenticeship papers yet, has he?"

"No. But I think he's about to, from what he said this morning." Martha turned the corners of her lips down and stuffed her fists onto her hips in an imitation of Baker Ames. "S'pose I might's well 'prentice you," she growled in a deep voice. "Hardly worth your keep, but at least I wouldn't have to start from scratch teaching you 'bout the bakery business, like I would a new 'prentice."

"Then there's no time to lose."

Martha yanked on Beth's sleeve. "What are you talking about?"

"Mary asked the seamstress Mrs. Brock whether she'd consider taking you as an apprentice. She said she'd talk to you tomorrow evening."

Martha stared at Beth. Her green eyes were wide, and her mouth formed a little O. Beth grinned at her surprise.

"Oh, Beth, truly?"

"Truly."

"But, where do I go? What do I do?"

"Mary said if you come to our house right after the evening meal tomorrow, she'll go with you to Mrs. Brock's. Mary says dress your best. Tell Mrs. Brock everything you know about sewing, and how much you want to be a seamstress." Beth paused to catch her breath. "You do want to be a seamstress, don't you?"

111

"I think it would be the loveliest way in the world to make a living!"

Beth wrinkled her nose. "Well, I don't. But I'm glad you think so."

"I can't wait to tell Mother."

"It's not definite, you know. I mean, Mrs. Brock hasn't said yes yet."

"I know. But I hadn't thought there was even a chance of something like this before."

"If Mrs. Brock likes you, your Mother will have to see her to agree on the apprenticeship terms."

Martha nodded so hard her red braid jerked up and down. Her brows knit together in a worried frown. "Do you think she'll like me?"

"Of course she will."

Martha smiled. "I hope so. Was this Mary's idea?"

Beth hesitated. "No, it was mine." She felt almost embarrassed admitting it.

Martha's smile grew wider. "Beth Smith, you are the best friend anyone ever had."

Her words made Beth all warm and funny inside. She'd never been able to do anything truly important for anyone before.

Why, I haven't seen Martha so happy, she realized, walking home a few minutes later. *Please, God, let Mrs. Brock like Martha very, very much.*

CHAPTER TWELVE
The Riot

Beth was so busy thinking about the happiness in Martha's face that she almost bumped right into Will and Tim in the middle of Cornhill street. She stopped so fast that Will had to grab her arm to keep her from falling.

Tim, as usual, laughed at her. "Clumsy Beth. You'll never change."

She just tossed her blonde curls behind her shoulder and ignored him. Even Tim couldn't ruin her good mood! "What are you two doing out? Shouldn't you be working in the shop on Mary's furniture?" All of the men had been working long hours since Mary's wedding had been announced.

Tim leaned closer. "Remember Millie?"

Of course she remembered their cow, Millie. What was he talking about?

Will gave her a friendly grin. "You forgot to bring Millie home from the common this evening, so Mother sent us to get her."

Beth slapped her hands to her cheeks. "Oh, no!" That was always her chore, unless her mother specially asked someone else to do it. "I can't believe I forgot!"

Tim sneered. "Your mind's getting as clumsy as your feet."

Will didn't give her a chance to make a smart reply back. "I guess you were so excited to tell Martha your news that you forgot all about Millie. What did Martha say?"

Beth told them, chattering eagerly while the three of them hurried along wide Cornhill Street with all its tall new buildings, up School Street, and along Common Street. As they passed the burying ground, Beth stopped talking. When she went by herself to take Millie to the common or bring her home, she took a different route. This way led by the almshouse, and she always tried to avoid that.

When they came to the large trees that sheltered the almshouse, Beth had to admit to herself that the house was built in a nice place. It was a quiet area, with the trees and the common to look out upon. There weren't houses and shops around like there were everywhere else in Boston.

Spinning wheels and stools were set out among the trees, and she realized that the women from the almshouse must have been working together outside in the pleasant weather. *It would be rather nice to have friends to work beside,* she thought. The hours spent spinning would surely go by much faster that way. Perhaps everything at the almshouse wasn't as bad as she'd thought.

She glanced about, looking for Mrs. Lankford and Sam, but didn't see them.

Just beyond the almshouse it wasn't peaceful at all. A large crowd, mostly men, were gathered on the rolling hills at the edge of the common. Someone was speaking—yelling, actually, in order to be heard. The crowd cheered the speaker and grumbled to each other as they listened.

They drew closer, forgetting Millie. What was happening?

"There must be two hundred people here!" Will said as they neared the group.

The speaker stood near the top of a small rise, where the crowd could see him best. His gray hair hung limp to his shoulders. Beth could tell even from this distance that his brown coat was shabby.

"Isn't that the man who yelled at Mr. Belcher in the courthouse?" she asked.

Will nodded. "I think so. Let's get closer where we can hear better."

They inched their way slowly through the crowd, dodging elbows as men shook angry fists in the air.

"Belcher sent ships of grain away in the past," the man was hollering, "and the selectmen we elected to protect our rights did nothing to stop him."

Shouts of "That's right!" "Selectmen don't care about us poor

115

people!" rose all around Beth and the boys.

"Belcher and the selectmen don't care whether you and your children go hungry!" the leader shouted.

"That's right!" "Tar and feather them!" the crowd cried.

Beth glanced at the men around her. A chill went through her. Their faces were screwed into angry expressions, eyes blazing. She inched closer to Will.

A man in a white wig and wearing an embroidered vest and fine long jacket stood beside the man with the brown coat. Beth gasped. "That's the lieutenant governor, Will! He's one of the most important men in Massachusetts. Why is he here?"

The lieutenant governor raised his arms, the cuffs on his coat reaching from his wrists almost to his elbows. "Good men, I beg you to listen to reason. Unlawful gatherings of this kind can lead only to trouble. Go home to your wives and children."

"I got a wife and children at home." Beth jumped as the man beside her yelled. He was a tall, muscular man in a leather craftsman's apron, and right now, he looked very mean. "But there's no bread at my house!"

"Yeah!" A man on the other side of Will took up the taunt. "Bet you have bread at your house, Gov! Want to invite us home for dinner?"

The lieutenant governor's face grew red. "If you won't go home, I'll have to call out the militia to break this up."

"I guess that means you're not invitin' us to share your bread!" the man beside Beth called out.

The man in the brown coat shoved the lieutenant governor roughly aside. "Think this man or the selectmen care if our children go hungry? All they care about is money!"

"That isn't true!"

Beth stared at the man who had just yelled. Was she seeing right?

"Josiah!" Will exclaimed. "What's he doing here?"

Josiah was walking across the top of the rise, his back straight, looking right at the crowd without any fear in his face. The waves of his wig bounced and the brass buttons on his green coat flashed as he walked. He stopped beside the man in the brown coat.

"The selectmen do care about your children," Josiah told the crowd. "They've been trying to buy grain for the town. There's none to buy."

"Belcher has grain!" the man beside him declared.

"You can't buy grain from a man who won't sell," Josiah said reasonably.

The mob leader stuck out his stubbly chin. "The selectmen should force him to sell."

Cries of agreement rose from the crowd.

"Would you want to be forced to sell your own property to whomever the selectmen said?" Josiah asked. "The government of Boston doesn't steal from its citizens, even if it believes they are acting unwisely."

"The selectmen don't have to steal," the man beside Beth shouted. "They can buy grain. I don't believe Belcher has the only grain left in Massachusetts!"

Beth's heart beat hard against her chest. The crowd's mood was getting uglier by the minute.

"The town's grain warehouse on this very common is probably filled with grain and corn," the man in the brown coat yelled back. "The selectmen and rich merchants are just keeping it all for themselves."

"That's not true!" the lieutenant governor cried.

"The warehouse is as empty as your own flour barrels," Josiah said.

The leader waved an impatient hand in their direction. "I say we break into the warehouse and find out for ourselves! Are you with me?"

The crowd roared and began moving toward the warehouse.

"Wait!" Beth heard Josiah yell while she hung on to Will's arm and tried to keep from being knocked over by the angry men. "Don't become lawbreakers! Speak with the selectmen and try to find an answer to this problem!"

"We've given the selectmen plenty of time," someone responded.

The crowd surged forward, eager now to reach the warehouse.

"Stop!" Josiah cried.

"Stop!" the lieutenant governor cried.

Suddenly rocks and sticks were flying through the air, and Josiah and the lieutenant governor were covering their faces with their arms to protect themselves.

A cold wave of fear swept Beth from her head to her feet. This couldn't be happening! Maybe it was one of her nightmares and she'd wake up any minute in her own safe bed.

But the nightmare only grew worse. Will pushed through the crowd to Josiah's side. He tried to help Josiah defend himself. Beth saw a rock bounce off Will's shoulder. She screamed and tried to push through the men to get to him.

"Think what you're doing!" Josiah cried desperately. Beth saw him and Will struggle to push back the men who swarmed around them as they headed for the warehouse. "You're not thieves!"

The crowd gathered force and speed. Beth had no choice but to move in the direction of Will and Josiah. There was no way to escape. The crowd carried her along in its anger, like a piece of driftwood carried by the Charles River. Out of the corner of her eye she saw Tim close by, being jostled about like she was.

By the time she reached Will, he and Josiah and the lieutenant governor were on the ground. The crowd was trying to separate to go around them, but because of the crush, not everyone was able to. People bumped into them, stepped on them, or tried to jump over them.

Desperate not to be swept past them, Beth flung herself down beside them.

Josiah threw an arm around her and dragged her close against his chest. "Beth, child! Keep her safe, Lord!" she heard him pray.

Will leaned close, trying to add the protection of his own body.

With them shielding her, Beth received only a few kicks. It seemed forever before the crowd of men had passed them by, though she knew it could only have been a few minutes.

Will straightened and Josiah released her. Beth sat up and looked at the men in horror.

The lieutenant governor was lying on the ground beside Josiah, groaning. His face and hands showed cuts, and his clothes were dirty.

Will was brushing his straight blond hair from his face. His clothes were torn and mussed. There was a large red spot on his cheekbone that seemed to be growing into a lump before her eyes.

"Are you all right?" Beth asked Will anxiously.

"I'm fine."

She touched the bruise on his cheek lightly. He flinched. "Sorry."

"Beth, let me look at you," Josiah demanded. "Have you been hurt?"

She shook her head. Her leg throbbed a bit where the crowd had kicked her, but she knew it wasn't more than a few bruises. She looked at Josiah and gasped.

Josiah's beautiful coat and his white breeches and silk stockings were filthy. His shoulder-length wig lay on the ground behind him, leaving his closely cropped hair revealed to the world. One arm—the arm that hadn't protected her, Beth realized—was twisted strangely.

"You've been hurt!" she cried.

He ignored her concern. "What were you two doing in this crowd? Don't you know how dangerous it is to be in the middle of a mob?"

For a moment she thought his stern face was white from anger. Then the lieutenant governor, trying to sit up, bumped his twisted arm, and she realized Josiah's face was white from pain.

Dread crawled through her stomach. "What's wrong with your arm?"

"I think it's broken." He tried to smile. "It was hit by a large rock. Someone in that crowd had very good aim."

Dusk was settling over the common. Beth could hear the crowd, still yelling, near the warehouse. Other sounds mingled with the yells. Were they tearing down the warehouse door?

Tim came running up behind them, panting. "I tried to get out of the crowd to help you, but I couldn't. Are you all right?" he asked, dropping to his knees beside Will.

It took him only a moment to see the shape everyone was in. His eyes grew huge.

Beth remembered how Tim had seemed to enjoy the townspeople's fury the last few weeks. He didn't look very happy over it now.

"We'd best get the lieutenant governor to his house," Josiah said, "and then get you children home. It's candle-lighting time. Your parents will be worried."

Beth was already worried. How could people in her own town have done such a thing? She'd thought when the ship's rudder had been cut and the people had wanted to force Mr. Belcher's ship to shore that things couldn't get much worse. But they had.

The people had hurt Will, Josiah, and the lieutenant governor, then hurried away without even checking to see how badly hurt they were.

If the selectmen couldn't find a way to help the people, would things get even worse?

Fear slithered through her.

CHAPTER THIRTEEN

Martha's Interview

When Martha arrived the following evening, it was Will who answered the door.

"What happened to you?" Beth heard Martha ask as she hurried into the entry hall.

"Doesn't he look awful?" Beth said before Will could answer.

The lump on his face had turned black and blue, and above it his eye was swollen almost shut. "Didn't you hear about the bread riot last night on the common?"

"I heard some people broke into the warehouse looking for grain, and that some people were hurt, but I didn't know you were hurt, Will."

"So was Josiah," Beth burst in again.

Then of course she and Will had to tell Martha everything.

"Father scolded us for being there, but he was proud of Will for helping Josiah. I could tell," Beth finished.

"Of course he was," Martha said promptly.

"Ah, it wasn't so much," Will said, scuffing at the floor with the toe of his shoe. "Any man would do the same for a friend."

"Not any man," Martha said quietly, "but they should."

Will's face grew red. He mumbled something about work to do on Mary's chairs and went into the shop.

Beth sat down on the bottom step of the stairs that led to the second floor. She wanted to tell Martha that she'd finished her new dress today, but she'd decided to wait until Martha and Mary were back from Mrs. Brock's. She almost had to bite her tongue to keep her promise to herself. Instead she said, "Do you know what the men found when they broke into the warehouse?"

Martha sat down beside her. "What?"

"Nothing." She waited a moment for her answer to sink in.

"Nothing?"

"There was no grain or corn left. Josiah told the crowd the truth when he said the town had no grain left to sell."

Martha's eyes grew large. "None?"

"None. Oh, and I almost forgot to tell you." Beth started laughing. "I was so eager to talk to you yesterday that I forgot to get

Millie from the common. That's why Will and Tim were there. But in all the excitement and trying to get Josiah and the lieutenant governor to their homes, we forgot Millie again! I had to go get her first thing this morning, before we even had breakfast!"

Martha smiled but didn't laugh. "Millie must have been glad to see you."

"She bawled me out good. She wanted to be milked!"

Something was wrong. Martha wasn't laughing at all. She was just staring at the floor, her fingers nervously playing with her skirt where it covered her knees.

Of course! She was probably nervous about her interview. "I'm sorry, Martha. I've been so excited about the bread riot that I didn't think about you being excited to see Mrs. Brock."

Martha's eyes filled with tears. "Oh, Beth, I don't think I can see Mrs. Brock tonight." She stood up and pulled her skirt about. "This is my best dress, and my only clean one. But I was in such a hurry this evening that I dropped some embers from the fireplace on it. Look."

A large, black-edged hole stood like a gash in the side of the skirt.

Beth's chest felt hot and tight. Martha was right, she couldn't go to Mrs. Brock's house like that. It wasn't fair! she raged inside. It wasn't fair that sweet Martha's plans had been ruined.

You could let her wear your new dress, a little voice seemed to say inside her head.

Beth swallowed hard. "You. . .you could wear my blue Sunday dress." That wasn't exactly what the voice in her head had said, but surely her blue dress would do. It was nicer than the dress Martha was wearing, even before she'd burned it, she told herself.

Martha's thin, freckled face brightened. "Do you mean it?"

Beth nodded. "Let's go to my room. You can change right away."

Beth couldn't get the picture of Mr. Belcher out of her mind while Martha changed. She'd been thinking about him a lot.

This morning Father had had Tim read the verses again about loving God and loving our neighbors as ourselves. Beth had said if Mr. Belcher had acted lovingly toward his neighbors and sold them grain and corn at prices they could afford, the people wouldn't have cut his ship's rudder or attacked the warehouse or hurt Will and Josiah. Her father had reminded her that the people who did those things hadn't acted lovingly either.

Would she act like Mr. Belcher if she had his grain? Would she sell it to the poor or sell it to someone who could give her more money for it? She wanted to think she would sell it to the poor, but would she? If she sold it for more money, she could have more and nicer dresses. Maybe she could even hire someone else to sew them!

Guilt wiggled through her. She shifted her feet uncomfortably and glanced at the large wooden cupboard. Her new dress hung inside on a peg. It was almost as if she could hear it scolding her for being so selfish.

She wasn't like Mr. Belcher. She wasn't!

"Beth, can you help me with this hoop? I can't get it tied on right."

Beth took a deep breath. "I don't think you should wear my old blue."

"But—"

Beth opened the cupboard door and removed her new yellow dress. "Mary and I just finished this today. I want you to wear it."

125

Martha gasped and reached out for the dress. She drew her hand back before touching it. "I couldn't. It's dear of you to offer it. I'll never forget it. But I couldn't. The blue will do fine."

"No, it won't. You have to look your best."

Martha smiled and shook her head.

"Please, Martha, I want you to wear it."

Martha hesitated. "But it's so beautiful." She slowly reached out to catch the material in her hands and spread the skirt wide, admiring it. "It's like a ray of sunshine."

"Let's see how you look in it."

When Martha was dressed, she turned all the way around for Beth. "Well?"

Beth tilted her head to one side. "Something is wrong." She put a finger to her cheek and studied her friend. "Your shoes. I haven't new shoes to lend you, but you can have my best pair."

Martha shook her head vigorously. "You've done too much already."

"Stop arguing with me. There's a hole in the toe of your shoe. A lot of people have holes in their shoes, what with how poor so many people are after Queen Anne's War and the Great Fire. But not everyone is seeing Mrs. Brock tonight. You don't want to embarrass Mary, do you?"

That settled it. Martha changed shoes.

"Now your hair. I have red ribbons to match the dress's ribbons. Would you like me to tie your hair back in one?"

When Martha's hair was brushed and tied, Beth was finally satisfied. "There's a looking glass in my parent's room."

Martha had to stand on Mr. and Mrs. Smith's feather bed in order to see all of herself in the looking glass. The soft mattress curled up around her feet. She teetered back and forth, trying to keep her balance.

Her friend's expression when she saw herself in the new dress made Beth glad she'd insisted Martha wear it. She couldn't remember ever seeing her look so happy.

"Don't let Mrs. Brock look at the stitching," Beth warned. "I'm not nearly as good a seamstress as you. If she sees my stitches, she'll never apprentice you!"

Martha laughed. "You've done a very good job on this dress. You're sewing has improved a lot."

Beth's cheeks grew hot, and her smile almost hurt her face it was so wide.

While Martha and Mary were gone, Beth watched Robert and worked on a new shirt for him. Martha's praise of her sewing made the work seem easier than usual.

She had a hard time keeping her mind on her work. She kept wondering how things were going with Martha and Mrs. Brock. *Please let Mrs. Brock like Martha,* she prayed over and over.

She was thinking so much of Martha that she forgot about Robert until Will brought him back to the sitting room from the shop. His dark breeches were covered in sawdust. One fat hand clutched curls of shaved wood with the outdoors smell of pine. "Look, Beth. Pretty."

"Yes, they're very pretty."

"Why?"

Beth rolled her eyes.

Will grinned. "Doesn't he ever get tired of asking that?"

"Never. I'm sorry I didn't see him go into the shop."

"That's all right. It's kind of nice to see him in there once in a while." He started back to the shop. "Pretty soon he won't be around to come into the shop."

She clutched her needle tightly. She'd almost forgotten. After the wedding, Robert wouldn't be here every day. She couldn't imagine what that would be like.

Robert leaned against her skirt. "Where's Mother?"

Beth sighed. She'd answered that question a dozen times already. "At Mrs. Brock's with Martha."

"Why?"

Beth shook her head and laughed. "Oh, no. Not again." She brushed the sawdust from his knee breeches. "Let's work on the Bible verse you're supposed to memorize this week."

Dusk was falling, and Beth lit the candles so she could see to keep working. They were still working on the verse and the shirt when Martha and Mary returned.

Beth jumped up from the rush bottomed chair. The forgotten shirt dropped to the floor. "I thought you'd never get back!"

The two just smiled and said hello.

Robert ran across the room and flung himself at his mother's knees. Mary knelt and hugged him.

"Well?" Beth demanded. "What did Mrs. Brock say?"

Martha's smile grew wider. "She said yes. Oh, Beth, she said yes!"

Beth grabbed Martha's hands. "I'm so glad for you!"

"Mrs. Brock complimented me on your dress. She said it was lovely."

Beth bit her lips, trying not to show how much the seamstress's compliment meant to her. But inside, she thought she'd burst from pride.

She pulled Martha over to the straight-backed chairs by the hearth. "Sit down, and then tell me everything!"

Martha laughed. "I was too nervous to remember everything. But I don't think Mrs. Brock would have wanted to apprentice me if it weren't for Mary." She glanced over at Mary, who was listening solemnly to Robert tell her all about the wood shavings he'd found in the shop. "She said the nicest things."

"Like what?"

"She told her that I'd helped her figure out how to stitch that new-style gown she was working on a few weeks ago, and that I'd stitched part of it."

Mary walked up to them with Robert in her arms. "Mrs. Brock remembered that she'd complimented me on how well that dress was made. She was impressed Martha is already such a skilled seamstress."

Martha squeezed Beth's hands. "I can't wait to tell Mother. She'll be so pleased. Mrs. Brock said I can stay at her house, but she didn't mention Mother and Sam." She bit her bottom lip. "I guess they'll have to stay at the almshouse."

Some of the happy light went out of Martha's eyes for a minute. Beth didn't know what to say to make her feel better.

"Mother says it's not as bad at the almshouse as we thought it would be. The worst thing is that it's crowded, so there isn't much privacy. She says it gets noisy sometimes, and she has to watch that Sam doesn't stray to the jail." Martha sighed. "Mostly, I guess I just miss her and Sam."

"Maybe they can visit you at Mrs. Brock's," Beth suggested.

"Maybe." She stood up. "I'd best change back to my own clothes. I don't want anything to happen to your wonderful dress before you have a chance to wear it yourself!"

While Martha was upstairs changing, Will and Charles came into the sitting room from the shop.

"We didn't want to ask in front of Martha in case it was bad news," Will said. "What happened at Mrs. Brock's?"

"She liked her!" Beth wanted to jump up and down with joy.

Mary smiled, rocking Robert on her hip. "Mrs. Brock wants to apprentice her."

Charles winked at Beth. "Looks like the Lord used you to answer your own prayer for Martha."

Beth stared at him. A sense of wonder filled her. Had God truly used her?

Will clapped a hand on the shoulder of her brown work dress. "Good for you, Beth."

She was a little uncomfortable at so much praise from Will and Charles. "I only asked Mary to speak to Mrs. Brock."

"You did more than that," Charles said quietly. "You changed Martha's life for the better."

Martha's slippers were flapping quickly against the wooden stairs, so Beth picked up a candle from the table beside her chair and hurried to the entry hall to meet her. The boys and Mary followed.

Martha's eyes were still shining. "It's dark already. I'd better hurry back. Baker Ames is sure to be upset that I've been gone so long."

"I'll light the lantern and walk with you," Charles offered, reaching for the wooden and glass lantern with its tallow candle that was kept on the table in the entry. "You shouldn't be out on the streets alone after dark."

He pushed up the glass on one side of the lantern. The edges of the glass squeaked as they slid against the wood. He used the candle Beth had brought from the sitting room to light the lantern candle.

"Have you told Baker Ames about Mrs. Brock yet?" Beth asked Martha.

"No. I'll have to tell him tomorrow. Mrs. Brock wants me to start next week."

Beth grinned. "Won't he be sorry he didn't apprentice you himself."

"I almost forgot!" Martha slapped her hands to her cheeks. "Baker Ames had the apprenticeship papers drawn up. They were delivered to the bakery today."

Fear wound through Beth's stomach. Will asked the question she couldn't get through her throat. "Did he sign them?"

Martha's cheeks grew so red that the color almost hid her freckles. "No. He doesn't know they arrived. He was busy when the clerk brought the package, so I took it. When I saw what it was, I was afraid he would sign it before I talked with Mrs. Brock. So I. . .I. . ." She bit her lip and looked from one to another.

"What did you do with it?" Will asked.

Martha wrung her hands together. "I shouldn't have done it."

"Done what?" Beth urged impatiently.

"I hid it in the flour."

The small entry hall rang with laughter.

CHAPTER FOURTEEN
Beth's New Roommates

Martha settled into her new position with Mrs. Brock easily and happily. Baker Ames had been furious when he found out about her apprenticeship, Martha confided, her eyes laughing.

But Mrs. Lankford had been very happy for her daughter. She came to Beth's house to thank her personally.

Mary quit her position with Mrs. Brock to concentrate on her own sewing. She told Beth that Josiah had promised her that after they married, Mrs. Brock and Martha would be hired to make all her gowns.

Beth wished all Boston was as happy as Martha and Mary. Since the people had broken into the warehouse on the common, the mood in the town had gone from angry to hopeless. With no grain in the town warehouse and Mr. Belcher refusing to sell grain, the people didn't know where to turn.

Beth and her family prayed every day for the Lord to provide an answer. Remembering that the Lord had answered her prayer for Martha gave Beth hope that He would answer the prayers for Boston's people, too.

The next couple weeks flew by as the family prepared for Mary's wedding. The bride's cakes were made, packed with fruit in order to use as little of the precious flour as possible. Beth thought her fingers would never stop being sore from holding a needle.

When the wedding day came, Mary was beautiful in a fashionable new gown of damask and lace. Josiah's outfit was elegant, trimmed with gold on the lapels and cuffs of his jacket, and on his long vest. His arm was in a sling, but Beth didn't think that detracted from his elegant look at all.

"It only reminds us how brave he was that night," she whispered to Will. Josiah's face was as stern and solemn as always, but it didn't seem cold to her anymore. She knew now what a good heart lay behind his strict nature.

Will, whose black-and-blue eye had faded to a nasty yellow, grinned and straightened the shoulders beneath the new jacket which came to his knees.

At the church, the governor performed the wedding. Beth knew some churches allowed pastors to perform weddings, but not the Puritans' churches. There was talk of a change. Some people thought it appropriate that God's ministers perform the ceremonies. It sounded like a nice idea to Beth, though she thought it would seem strange at first.

After the vows, the Reverend Cotton Mather gave a sermon, and a prayer was offered.

Then came the walking out of the bride. Josiah and Mary led the six couples in their wedding party through the streets to Josiah's fine home.

Beth wore her new dress and slippers for the wedding and smiled broadly at all the compliments she received.

When all the excitement of the wedding was over, Robert went home with Josiah and Mary to Josiah's new home. The Smith house was strangely quiet now. For Beth, the days grew long without Robert to watch while she did her chores.

One night soon after the wedding, Josiah, Mary, Robert, and Josiah's year-old son, Thomas, joined them for dinner. Beth thought it was wonderful to have Mary and Robert with them again, even for such a short time. It looked sweet to see Mary holding little Thomas and stern-faced Josiah bouncing Robert on his knee.

Mary's blue eyes twinkled. "Josiah has wonderful news. It will be all over town tomorrow, but I want my family to hear it first."

Josiah smiled at her. "I spoke to the selectmen and suggested they ban the export of grain. They voted tonight to do so. They cannot force Belcher to sell to the townspeople at good prices, but the law will allow them to keep him from sending the grain away. Our hope is that when he finds he can't sell it elsewhere, he will sell it here, at whatever the people can pay."

"Good," Tim said fiercely.

Since Will and Josiah had been hurt in the bread riot, Tim had changed. He was quieter and didn't talk boldly about the right of the people to take what they needed anymore. Beth thought it was because he'd learned that people could truly be hurt by such actions.

"Tell them the rest, Josiah," Mary urged.

"The selectmen are sending someone to the southern colonies to try to purchase grain there. If they are successful, the select-men will see the grain is available to the townspeople."

"That's wonderful!" Father beamed.

"It sounds as though God is answering our prayers," Mother said.

Mary smiled over Thomas's head. "That was Josiah's idea, too."

Beth studied Josiah. When she'd first met him, she'd thought of him as a cold, wealthy young man. But she'd found him to be brave, with a kind heart, and now she knew he was intelligent and wise, too. She could see why Mary was so fond of him.

The house seemed very quiet when the Foy family left, as it had every day since the wedding.

Beth sat on a stool beside her mother's chair and listened to her father read the Bible. When prayer was over, she propped her elbows on her knees and rested her chin in her hands. "I used to think I would like it when I didn't have to look after Robert anymore and when I had my room to myself."

"Don't you?" her mother asked gently.

Beth was a little embarrassed when she realized everyone in the room was watching her. "No. I miss Mary and Robert."

135

"We all do," Will said.

"Yes," her father said. "But that's the way life is meant to be. Children grow up and move away from their parents' homes."

"I know. But I was thinking. . ." Beth paused, not knowing how to continue. What if her parents said no?

"Tell us, Beth," her father urged.

"Could Mrs. Lankford and Samuel come to live with us?"

Her father and mother exchanged dismayed glances.

"They could sleep in my room with me. I'm used to Mary and Robert sharing the room, so it wouldn't seem crowded," Beth pleaded. She held her breath. She wanted so badly for them to say yes!

Her mother pushed a stray gray hair behind her ear. "That's a big decision."

"It's kind of you to want them," her father started, "but to ask another family to stay. . ." He shook his head. "I just don't know."

Beth leaned forward, as if she could change their minds just by the force of her desire. "But you've told us to love our neighbors as ourselves."

"It isn't necessarily loving to take people into our home. We must be sure we can provide for them," Father reminded her.

"But they won't eat any more than Mary and Robert did," Beth argued. "And Mrs. Lankford can help around the house. Maybe when she's stronger she can find work."

Father and Mother exchanged glances again across the room. "It might mean waiting even longer than we've planned to build a new shop," he said to her mother. "You won't have your parlor back for a long time."

Mother leaned against the tall back of the chair and smiled. "It is rather nice with you and Will across the hall all day long, instead of blocks away at a shop."

Beth bit her lips hard together. Was there a chance?

Father raised an eyebrow, silently asking his wife what she thought.

Mother gave one sharp nod.

"Would you like to ask them tomorrow if they will move in with us, Beth?" Father asked.

She flung herself into his arms. "Oh, Father, thank you!"

Next she hugged her mother and thanked her, too.

"I'll never be able to sleep tonight," she said to Will as they walked upstairs to their bedrooms together, the candles they carried throwing wavering shadows on the wall.

Will stopped at the door of his room. "You know, for a sister, you're pretty good." He opened the door and grinned. "Matter of fact, I'm proud of the woman you've become."

She stared at the door he closed behind him. Then she opened the door to her own room. The candlelight chased away the darkness inside. She smiled as she set the candle down on the table beside her bed. "Thank You, Lord," she whispered.

A woman, she thought. A smile crept across her heart as she slipped between the covers.

Good News for Readers

There's more! The American Adventure continues in *Smallpox Strikes!*

Rob Allerton has problems. His stepfather, Josiah Foy, is determined to make a shipping clerk out of him, but Rob hates everything about the family business. And when he isn't getting in trouble at work, Rob and his half-sister Rachel are being set up for trouble at home by their stepbrother, Thomas. Then on top of everything else, smallpox breaks out in Boston.

Rob's friend Dr. Boylston has a radical new treatment that may save people from the horrible disease, but Josiah refuses to even consider letting his family be inoculated. Can Rob convince his step-father to risk Dr. Boylston's treatment before the family contracts this deadly disease?

Books for ages 7 to 12

Kid Stuff
Fun-filled Activity Books for ages 7-12

Bible Questions and Answers for Kids
Collection #1 and #2

Brain-teasing questions and answers from the Bible are sure to satisfy the curiosity of any kid. And fun illustrations combined with Bible trivia make for great entertainment and learning! Trade paper; 8 ½" x 11" $2.97 each.

Bible Crosswords for Kids
Collection #1 and #2

Two great collections of Bible-based crossword puzzles are sure to challenge kids ages seven to twelve. Hours of enjoyment and Bible learning are combined into these terrific activity books. Trade paper; 8 ½" x 11" $2.97 each.

The Kid's Book of Awesome Bible Activities
Collection #1 and #2

These fun-filled, Bible-based activity books include challenging word searches, puzzles, hidden pictures, and more! Bible learning becomes fun and meaningful with *The Kid's Book of Awesome Bible Activities.* Trade paper; 8 ½" x 11" $2.97 each.

Available wherever books are sold.
Or order from:
Barbour & Company, Inc.
P.O. Box 719
Uhrichsville, Ohio 44683
http://www.barbourbooks.com

If you order by mail, add $2.00 to your order for shipping. Prices subject to change without notice.

Juli Scott Super Sleuth

*A mystery series for girls ages 9-15
by Colleen L. Reece*

If you love mysteries, then you'll devour these brand new books in the Juli Scott Super Sleuth series! Nail-biting excitement and adventure await in *Mysterious Monday* and *Trouble on Tuesday* as Juli and her savvy friends sort out the clues and solve each mystery. But wait! It gets even better. . .this mystery series includes a clear Christian message throughout each book.

Mysterious Monday
Sophomore Juli Scott can't accept her father's death. Something deep inside her refuses to believe policeman Gary Scott was killed in the line of duty. The case has been closed but left unresolved by the police department, and Juli is determined to resolve it herself. In a series of events, Juli and her friends are plunged into excitement, adventure, and terrible danger. Trade paper. $2.97.

Trouble on Tuesday
A fortune teller, a crystal ball, an uncanny prediction, and a self-proclaimed prophet named Lord Leopold trap Juli Scott's best friend, Shannon, in a web of deceit. In spite of everything her friends do to help, only God will be able to save Shannon from a frightening cult that threatens to destroy both her mind and soul. Trade paper. $2.97.

Available wherever books are sold.
Or order from:
Barbour & Company, Inc.

P.O. Box 719

Uhrichsville, Ohio 44683

http://www.barbourbooks.com

If you order by mail, add $2.00 to your order for shipping. Prices subject to change without notice.